The people who met the Gypsy were many, and varied. Their histories, their social conditions, the times in which they lived, all differed.

Mother Mary Joseph was a woman of God, but she was moved by the gentle power of the Gypsy. So, too, was Robert Younge, a fiery young Elizabethan exiled for killing one of the Queen's favourites. And after him came many others, an Arctic whaler, a French emigré, a Chinese missionary – all strangely influenced by their encounters with the Gypsy . . .

Also by Norah Lofts

JASSY
THE BRITTLE GLASS
A CALF FOR VENUS
QUEEN IN WAITING
SCENT OF CLOVES
THE LUTE PLAYER
BLESS THIS HOUSE
THE DEVIL IN CLEVELY
OUT OF THIS NETTLE
TO SEE A FINE LADY
THE ROAD TO REVELATION
HESTER ROON
MADSELIN
HERE WAS A MAN
BLOSSOM LIKE THE ROSE
WHITE HELL OF PITY
THE LOST QUEEN
HOW FAR TO BETHLEHEM
THE CONCUBINE
REQUIEM FOR IDOLS
HEAVEN IN YOUR HAND
HER OWN SPECIAL ISLAND
ESTHER
IS THERE ANYBODY THERE?

The House Trilogy
THE TOWN HOUSE
THE HOUSE AT OLD VINE
THE HOUSE AT SUNSET

Norah Lofts writing as Peter Curtis
DEAD MARCH IN THREE KEYS
YOU'RE BEST ALONE
THE LITTLE WAX DOLL

and published by Corgi Books

Norah Lofts

I Met a Gypsy

CORGI BOOKS
A DIVISION OF TRANSWORLD PUBLISHERS LTD

I MET A GYPSY

A CORGI BOOK 0 552 10725 5

Originally published in Great Britain
by Methuen & Co. Ltd.

PRINTING HISTORY
Methuen edition published 1935
Corgi edition published 1970
Corgi edition reprinted 1972
Corgi edition reissued 1978

This book is set in 11 pt Georgian

Corgi Books are published by Transworld Publishers Ltd.,
Century House, 61–63 Uxbridge Road, Ealing,
London W5 5SA
Made and printed in Great Britain by
Cox & Wyman Ltd.,
London, Reading and Fakenham

Contents

MOTHER MARY JOSEPH TELLS THE STORY OF THE BRIDE OF CHRIST A.D. 1536

CHAPTER ONE

BRIDE OF CHRIST

It is, my children, all a very great mystery, not less so to me who am old than to you who are young. Some things we know to be right, others wrong, but there are many things so dependent upon the circumstances and the people concerned that what seems wrong may well be right, and that which we hope to be right may not be so. And even an impulse which comes as if it were the voice of God in pity for our weariness, may equally be the voice of the Devil, seeing in our uncertainty his dreadful opportunity. Now in my age I can look back upon a long line of actions; the results of some of them are plainly before me for my joy or sorrow, others are hidden – and that may well be God's mercy. There is one of my actions. . . .

If the old order were still with us and I indeed your mother and you my children, I should hesitate to tell you this story; but since the world has engulfed us all and the old order has gone, never, I fear, to return, I can tell you the story of a decision of mine. Its consequences are hidden from me, but they may endure and increase, even as long as there is life upon this earth.

It concerns one whom I had known all her life, for she was born in the Convent Hospitium some twenty years before the trouble came upon us. Her mother was a mere wandering gypsy whose hour had come upon her at our very doors; the father, if indeed the woman spoke truth, and I cannot see what service a lie could do her in her evil case – I had better not mention, even at this hour. Indeed, he was so great a temporal Lord that I was moved to believe the woman; for otherwise how would she have known him well enough to describe him so faithfully, as she did both in her delirium and in her few quiet moments? Despite our care she died, and the babe remained with four or five other unfortunates whom we endeavoured to rear as befitted God's children.

The years passed and the child grew apace and early showed many tendencies that we could only regret. She was wild and rough, domineering with her fellows, intolerant of restraint, disrespectful often to her elders. The Sisters would excuse her one to another, so that often the one who had most cause for offence would be foremost in shielding her from the just punishment that she merited. Because she was no one's child she became the child of everyone and was, I fear, sadly spoiled. She had, moreover, a wild grace of manner which exerted particular charm in a world where it was rare, and she was beautiful as a young flower or a small animal is beautiful. So that I no less than the others remembered as often as might be that wild blood ran in her veins from at least one source that we knew of and perchance from another too.

At length the time came when we must decide upon her future, and I and the five or six that loved her despite her follies were sorely exercised in our mind for her. We wanted to keep her with us in safety, yet she had little vocation, none indeed that I could perceive. She was nimble with her feet, her fingers, and her tongue; she might, I felt, have been useful and successful in the world, and yet she was passing lovely, hot of blood, and high of heart, and I feared for her, remembering also her mother. And when in her seventeenth year she entered at her own wish upon her novitiate, I was eased in heart and glad to have added so fair a flower to Heaven's garden; for I hold that not only the old and tired or the ill-favoured or those broken upon the wheels of life should be offered specially as our Lord's brides.

Yet even after that I was at times troubled. Frequently I would see her, when she thought herself to be unobserved, studying her face in a night-backed window or in the candlesticks and chalices as she polished them; and many a time Sister Thomasina had to rebuke her for overmuch chatter to travellers whom we sheltered for the night, or for lingering at the door when any stir was afoot. And one night when the moon was in the garden, and the scent of the lilac heavy on the night, I found her pressing her face into the white flowers and weeping without restraint. To my questions as to what troubled her she made no answer . . . and I remembered that long before I gave up the world I too had found strange sorrow in the night, the moon, and the flowers and had yearned for many things which God in His great wisdom saw fit to deny me. This of course I could tell not her, but I said: 'Go in, my daughter,' and set her some light task. And I must in justice add that any task assigned her was well and truly perormed; even the silver was not the less bright because she used it for a mirror.

She took the veil at the beginning of the year that the trouble came upon us. It was in accordance with her own wish; and yet on the day of her reception I, who had seen many such days, was sad and knew not why. Surely, I said, the more the heart turns towards the world, the more need to renounce it; the more obdurate the spirit, the more need to subdue it.

From that time she was changed indeed; she walked and spoke more humbly, lingered less over the duties that brought her into contact with the outer world, and was ever eager for the harder and less agreeable of the Sisters' tasks. And then, as you know, after our hopes and our fears had had alternately the upper place in our hearts, the King's commissioners came. I was asked in great detail an account of my stewardship. There were eighty questions that must be answered in great haste, there were many things to show. It was a lengthy business, and when they had gone, to return, they told me, in the morning, I went into the chapel to regain the calm that I had so sadly lost during the day. When I returned, Beatrice, for so we called her, was waiting with a request to speak with me, I gave her permission to speak and to be seated, but she stood dumb for a while, twisting her hands in her girdle and looking down at my feet.

'I am waiting, my daughter,' I said.

'Mother,' she began, 'may I speak frankly?'

'Assuredly,' I said; 'how else would you?'

Then she began. I will not weary you by repeating her sayings word for word, though I remember each one clearly, her speech and her manner so graved themselves upon my mind. She told me that the year's end would find the convent closed, the nuns scattered, the lands divided. All that and much more she said; indeed the spirit of the old prophets might have been upon her tongue, crying as it were: 'Woe unto Jerusalem!' Only at the time I did not know this. I listened and then I said:

'And if, my daughter, it should please God to lay this heavy trouble upon His people, our foreknowledge can do us no good; it remains only for us to show patience and fortitude.'

But at that she came and leaned upon my table, so that I looked straight into her eyes, noting anew their clear pale glitter:

'You need not go empty, Mother, when the time arrives for going. These men are making assessment of all that we have; the lands they may measure, the stones they may count, the chalices and clothes and pictures they may reckon, but the coins – no. There is money in the strong-box, money in the alms-bags; hide that, my Mother, while you may, so that the evil day that is surely coming may find you at least provided against hunger.'

I was grieved to the heart to see that the world was so strong in her that she imagined that I could use the coins of charity in such a way, and I said gravely:

'My daughter, when our Lord was very hungry in the wilderness, He was tempted not with base coins but with sweet bread, and yet He sinned not; let us at least renounce the idea of sinning to provide for the hunger that is yet to come.'

And then she said, with such passion that I was aghast:

'There is also the story of the Unjust Steward.'

Then I saw that this new fashion of questioning and arguing had influenced even Christ's own.

'That is enough,' I cried; 'tomorrow you will repent of this your waywardness. Employ that repentance well.'

'And tomorrow you will tell them everything?' she asked.

'Tomorrow,' I said, 'I shall endeavour to act as God would have me. See that you do likewise.'

At that she left me, going out staring as if before her she could see things invisible, and still twisting her fingers in the cord at her waist.

The business was concluded, and at the year's end the soldiers came and we were ordered forth just as she had said. We held a conference amongst ourselves, and knowing that the house at Welland was still standing and undisturbed, and having the King's permission to go there, we decided to leave on the morrow in the morning together. At the end, when the thought of leaving had pierced every heart and we were all in tears, Beatrice, who alone was not crying, spoke out without permission and before her elders without fear.

'Why hide from the truth for a further year?' she asked. 'Think you that Henry Tudor will take the little and spare the great, spoil the poor and leave the rich? A month, two, six at the very most, and the King's soldiers will be hammering upon that door as they have upon this.'

I was about to rebuke her again, for at her words a new storm of tears shook all the Sisters, but I remembered that she had told me aright before, so I said as gently as I could:

'Those who decry other people's counsel should be prepared not to judge only, but to improve. Is that possible? What better plan have you?'

On that question a perfect torrent of words poured from her lips.

'We have all hands, and eyes, and a portion of strength according to our state. We could find work in the world. Sister Thomasina, who does such beautiful embroidery for the church, could she not make shifts and smocks? Who can grow flowers can grow corn, who can make simples to give to the sick poor can make simples to sell to the sick who are not so poor. We can scour and bake and brew; better to face it of choice than of necessity in a year's time, when we are all a year older and the roads are crowded with women from the bigger houses offering the same wares for sale.'

There was, I realized, a strange truth in her word, and conviction upon her tongue, and I marvelled at her knowledge of a world in which she had never lived. But I said:

'The King is exceedingly powerful; he has made himself head of the Church, but he is not God. He cannot cancel a vow that was made to God alone. Did you, when you took your vows, stipulate that it was only for the time during which we remained here, or were they made for all time? Even if I were sure that all the ill you predict were certain to come, that would not make me less a nun, whose proper home, while one is standing, is a convent.' With this the rest agreed and Beatrice said no more; but I saw her stare at me as if I had said something strange and hard to understand, instead of something so simple that it seemed unnecessary to put it into words.

The morning came, a morning of heavy sorrow for us all; the great gates were opened, and the portress's lodge stood at last empty. The rough voices of the soldiers struck echoes from the groining of our roofs; the nails in their boots clattered on our stone floors and sent out sparks; ribald jests and coarse laughter resounded in the chapel, where only sacred words and music had hitherto been heard. We gathered together, Francesca holding the cat, that struggled, poor thing, wondering why its happy stalking of sparrows in the ivy should be so suddenly disturbed. Beatrice was missing, and I realized that I was not surprised; I did not, however, deter poor Thomasina, who had ever loved even as she rebuked her, from running about calling 'Beatrice,' in a voice thick with tears. The others joined her, and little Francesca in a voice like a startled bird's went crying: 'Beatrice' so heartbrokenly that at last I bade them cease.

Outside, a crowd had gathered to watch the soldiers, who held them at a distance with oaths and curses, and a few in the crowd, more faithful or with better memories than others, pressed upon us little gifts for our better ease on the journey. But the majority stood with blank faces, some not even offering to move aside that we might pass, for the King's hostile attitude had influenced his subjects. We walked quickly, for Welland was a day and a half's journey distant, and the autumn had come, so that night would overtake us early – night, which for the first time would find us without a roof between us and the sky.

The road was nothing more than a track worn by the feet of passers-by and pack-horses. I wished indeed that Welland had been west of us; then we could have followed the highway and seen other people making the journey, and perhaps even have found some faithful soul who would have offered us the shelter of a barn or kitchen. On this track we saw no one except a woman driving a flock of geese up to London for the Christmas season. The geese had had their feet dipped in tar, so that each trod in a pair of little black boots; we looked at them with interest, never having seen the like before. On either hand the autumn woods blazed in the brief midday sun; we panted as we hurried along, and the cat was passed from hand to hand as she who carried it grew weary. We had brought bread with us and we ate it after saying grace in as orderly fashion as we could, then hurried on again. At last the shadows deepened and met across the road, and we were contemplating turning aside into the woods and sleeping on the leaves. That seemed at the moment to our unaccustomed minds a sorry prospect, but a few seconds later it seemed to us looking back at it like a prospect of paradise.

For suddenly the shadows took shape and substance and we found ourselves surrounded by a band of wild, fierce men. You, my children, live in a time when sturdy beggars are much put down and discouraged, but at the time of which I speak great bands of them roamed the roads and they were much feared and very seldom punished. Many of them were indeed hungry, workless, and desperate men to whom much must be forgiven, but they had been joined by wild and lawless boys who, being young, were influenced by Henry Tudor's lack of reverence for holy things; and of these most unfortunately was the band that accosted us composed.

As the elder and superior it behoved me to show an example of dignity and courage, and this I tried to do, explaining in simple words that we had with us nothing of value, that we were indeed so poor that we were reduced to spending the night under the trees. It was no good. Alas, like the King, they had only to see a habit to imagine that gold was hidden beneath it, and despite our protests and cries and entreaties they laid their marauding hands upon us and tore our clothing, snatching at our rosaries only to fling them aside cursing when they found that they were indeed worthless, as I had said. Then worse befell us – our defencelessness had awakened feelings more evil than cupidity, if you can understand that, my children. Shame even after all these years forbids me to repeat all that they said; sufficient to say that they too were going to spend the night under the trees ... and with us. At least, cried one, we were all women and some of untried virginity. And at that the hands ceased to be merely the dirty groping hands of robbers and became the dreadful claws of satyrs. We tried to escape, we pleaded, even wept, but it was no use, our cries could bring no passer-by to help, for only God could save us.

And that He did, for as our last despairing cries faded into the night, there came other louder cries from the woods, and suddenly bursting out of the bushes came another band, this time men and women, and the foremost woman of them all was our lost nun, Beatrice. She had discarded her veil and wore already the gaudy, dirty cloth that the female gypsy wears, her habit was kilted to the knee, and in her hand she brandished a great gnarled stick, like the monks who, habit to knee and staff in hand, stood by Harold at Senlac. She made straight at the robber who was holding me and caught him a crashing blow across the face. Our enemies had not troubled to brandish their weapons against us women, so they were taken unawares by the tumbling, shrieking attack of Beatrice and her followers. These were true gypsies of the kind whom the casual beggars both hate and fear, and with a few shouts and half-hearted blows our enemies disappeared into the shadows on the other side of the road. So far and for the moment we were saved, but the faces now surrounding us were of little improvement upon the others and perhaps we showed our dismay, for Beatrice said reassuringly: 'Have no fear, my Mother, these are my people, friends.' And indeed the gypsies with every appearance of friendliness were brushing down our dishevelled garments and collecting the scattered beads of our rosaries. Beatrice continued:

'I have been near you all day, following along paths through the woods that only these use. I was greatly feared for you, my Mother. Now, if you will come along with us for the night, we will see you safely to your journey's end tomorrow.'

'We shall be glad to do so,' I answered; for indeed I had forgotten that even poor women were not safe alone in the world and I shuddered anew at the memory of the awful fate we had so narrowly escaped. Beatrice went aside to speak to a man with a huge, black, tangled beard, who seemed to be the gypsy leader, and we all turned aside and made our way into the woods. In a very short time we stopped and, as if by magic, a fire grew up, a great leaping fire that lit up the trunks of the trees. At it the gypsies roasted salted herrings, and of these and fat pork and coarse brown bread we made a hearty supper. Apart from the fact that they served us, their guests, with courteous attention, their manners were deplorable; they tore at their food and made noises over it like animals; but they were kind and thoughtful, making us up beds of leaves near to the fire and leaving us there in decent privacy. Beatrice lay down by herself with neither party; throughout the supper she had behaved with this same detachment, as it were shrinking from joining us. When all was still, I called her to me.

'We owe you more than we can ever thank you for,' I said, 'but I do not understand. You call these your people, but how and where did you find them? How above all do you have such power over them that they spend a whole day following us at your bidding?'

I saw, by the dying glow of the fire, that a deep blush crept up from her neck, and she was silent for some moments and held her eyes averted; then she turned towards me and raised her eyes, so that, as once before, I was gazing into their clear depths:

'By means of a great sin, my Mother, by the promise of gold from the alms-bag.' And from the bosom of her habit she drew out and showed me the well-known canvas bag.

'I stole it; I meant to set up an ale-house for myself; I hid in the cellar. Many people called me, but not you; I thought that you understood and would forgive me. And then I saw you set off, so helpless to undertake so perilous a road, and instead, when I met them as I had arranged, I bribed them to come with me Wellandwards – that is all.'

Now for a little I too was silent, for though she had like Judas laid greedy hands upon charity's alms, she had by that same action saved us from undying shame.

'As you have arranged, you say. I am strangely curious to know how you made these arrangements, and when and why were you not content?'

'I have been in touch with the gypsies ever since the night when the commissioners came, when I spoke to you, Mother; I had listened and considered. . . .'

'And the world has been calling you, Beatrice, ever since the lilac's blooming these three years past. Why? Tell me that.'

'It is a hard thing to say to you, for you are holy. But I want to live, Mother, and this seemed the chance for which I had longed and waited.'

'And do you think that you can live more fully than in God's service, in our Lord's blessing, with your thoughts turned ever heavenwards?'

'It is a fair world, with many things to see and learn and know. Too fair to renounce, I thought, without ever having known it. But I was wrong. Oh, I have sinned in my heart many times, longing for forbidden things, and I have sinned grievously in taking what was not mine; but do you, I pray you, forgive me. Take me with you tomorrow, and I will do any penance each and every day until such time as you shall think me worthy of absolution. And I will think of the world no more as a fair place, Mother, but as the place where impious hands are laid upon Christ's own, and where their safety is only bought with stolen gold.'

Throughout her speech her voice had become more and more unsteady, and now she wept, with far more bitterness than there was in any of the tears with which we had received the evil tidings of our dissolution. I said at last:

'Leave me now, my daughter. I will think of you and pray about the matter, and will have more speech with you in the morning. Go in peace.'

Still sobbing she crept away to her own place, and I lay upon that heap of dried and crumpling leaves and watched the moon rise and set; then I knelt and begged God's guidance in this matter of His own, yet I saw no clear path. All that I had learned and experienced bade me take her with us and urge her to remain true to her vows, but I was afraid. Many doubtless have been dragged into heaven despite themselves, but it seemed to me an unworthy, unlovely progress. The stars paled, the moon set, and very early the gypsies were afoot, raking together the red ashes of the fire, feeding it with dry twigs and leaves; and presently with our escort we set out upon the last stage of our journey. The road grew worse and I began to feel the burden of my years and my infirmity. Then presently Beatrice stole to my side and said softly:

'The road is rough, lean upon me, my Mother.' She moved the cat on to her other arm and I put my hand upon her shoulder, savouring for the first time in many years the warmth and comfortable support of another's body. At midday the towers and gates of Welland came into view through the trees, and from farther east came the cool breezes and distant murmur of the North Sea. The nuns were silent, but the gypsies were chattering amongst themselves, using many words which we did not understand, and some of the children, ragged, tousled, but happy little creatures, ran with shouts alongside. I stopped and drew Beatrice a little aside. She looked at me earnestly, the sun shining in her eyes, making them clearer and greener than the glass in our east window. While I was still searching for words, she took the bag again from her bosom.

'It must be theirs because of the promise, but I will repay it all somehow. Have I your permission to give it to their leader?'

And I said: 'My daughter, the affairs of the world and of our Holy Mother Church have come to a strange pass. All that you told me of this disaster came to pass, and all that you foretell may with God's permission yet befall us; we may all be shaken into the world together. To you now it seems a place where your strength and talents may yet be useful. The voice which calls you so clearly may be indeed God's. I pray it may be so and that in learning and knowing the things that seem good to you you may yet serve Him. I do not know. I feel at the moment only an old woman who sees the things she has believed in, the very boundaries of her life, crumbling away. I tell you to go. Reckon not overmuch with the world; forget not your prayers and your duties, nor the fact that all our lives, whether within consecrated walls or without, are equally in God's sight and accountable to Him. And we, for our part, will not forget that we owe you more than our poor lives. We will remember you in our prayers. As for the money, that responsibility shall be mine. Go in peace, my child.'

Then Thomasina and Francesca and Teresa lifted up their voices and wept, and there was a chorus of broken voices saying: 'God bless you' and 'Go in peace.' She went back with the bag in her hand to the place where the gypsies had halted, and we turned to ring the bell at the great gate of Welland. I remembered how I had said that Henry Tudor could not absolve vows made to God alone, yet I myself had bid her go. I looked back and saw one of the children, weary from much running hither and thither, lift its arms towards her; she stooped and lifted it to her shoulder. Was I right or wrong? How could I even begin to know? As I stepped across the threshold I prayed that any good she might do in the world might go to her credit, and the evil, if any, be laid to my charge ... if God could not forgive.

ROBERT YOUNGE, ESQ., OF LONGMERE
IN THE COUNTY OF NORFOLK,
TELLS THE STORY OF
THE TRIAL BY FIRE A.D. 1600

CHAPTER TWO

THE SLAVE

My father took up his long new pipe and began to fill it without looking at me. I stood waiting for the wrath that I knew would soon be poured upon my head. I forgot in that one horrible moment of anticipation that I was a man, that I had lived in London, that I knew many famous men, that I could make verses; all these little things upon which I had prided myself fled away. Even the big thing, the fact that I had killed a man, was no longer a tribute to my skill, or coolness, or courage. It became instead the major charge in the indictment that I now awaited. And none came, for my father said calmly:

'There seems but one thing to do, and that is to get you out of England as quickly as we can. If you stay here, the Queen will never rest till you join Dick Fairfax underground; and a rope across your horse's path or a knife between your shoulder-blades some dark night is not an end I covet for my heir.'

He pondered a little, and then said:

'Markham's the man, and if he hasn't set sail from Yarmouth yet, with him you shall go. We'd better get off at once.'

'But,' I said, 'to go at once is impossible, I must see her once . . . if only to say good-bye.'

'Oh yes,' he said, in the dry voice that I hated; 'if you did go to see her it would be good-bye. Do you think the Queen's men will ever be away from her doorstep? You've been a fool, my boy, as better men before you have been; now is your time to listen to an old campaigner. You've risked your life once in the cause of a pretty face, and that will suffice for the moment.'

And so, without a word of comfort to me, he went out and I heard him giving orders to saddle the horses immediately. Thus it was that I left my beloved Longmere and Diana, even more beloved because less mine, and set out on the journey that was to show me many things, and send me home a wiser, if not a better man. I can look back now and smile at the pretty conceit of a boy scarcely bearded, that had led me to call out and meet and kill one of Elizabeth Tudor's favourites, because in my hearing he had spoken lightly of a woman whose very name had been known to me but a brief month.

We rode as hard as we dared through the soft spring darkness, for the time of the singing of the birds had come indeed, that loveliest time when under the young leaves of my Longmere woods the oxlips were all aflower, and the long grass in our orchard was yellow with daffodils. The thought of those daffodils made me groan inwardly as I rode, for it brought before me the realization of all the other things I was leaving. The Globe where we had gone hot-foot for Will Shakspere's plays, and the books in which we had read again lingeringly the words that had pleased as they fell from Burbage's lips. ... 'When wheat is green, when hawthorn buds appear.' No matter where or when I read that I could see the young wheat, ruffled into waves by the wind, and the green mist thickening over the black and knotted branches. None of this could I tell my father, so we rode with the silence heavy between us, and at last the cobbles rang under our horses's hoofs. Lifting his head, he said: 'Thank God, she's still there. Look, Robert, there's the *Firebird* that's going to do that doting old woman out of her revenge.'

I heard the note of relief in his voice and realized that he loved me and my escapade, and that the consequent danger had given him severe, if brief, concern. So I crushed back the rebellious words that rose to my tongue, went meekly aboard behind him, and was handed like a parcel to Captain Markham's care. My father had a short hurried talk with him, gave him money, and then came to me and put his hand upon my shoulder.

'You'll be gone a long time, my boy, eighteen months perhaps or two years. I'm sorry for it and if there was time to search out a ship bound for a shorter voyage we'd do it, for the Queen can hardly live so long. But time is short. So good-bye, Robert, and remember ... when your dreams fade and desire pricks, don't have another man's leavings.' And so he went away very briskly, leaving me with a hot blush upon my face.

I carried my few things below into my cabin, obeying the Captain's order to keep out of sight until we sailed, which would be soon. I found the cabin to be a narrow, airless cell in which I could just stand upright. Its door was at an angle to another door exactly like it, and as I laid out my clothes and the precious folios, miserably conscious that I was preparing for two years' solitary imprisonment, the door opposite was opened and a man appeared. I could see as I glanced cautiously over my shoulder that he stood lounging against the doorpost, looking very fixedly at me. My heart began to beat rapidly – surely, surely she had not sent after me already. I remembered that men credited her with superhuman powers. I wished that I had thought to shut my door; to do it now, I must turn and face him. I thought of dear Will again – 'Conscience doth make cowards of us all' – and turned. The stranger smiled and came forward a step so that he now leaned against my doorpost.

'I had not hoped,' he said in a clear, ringing voice, 'to have any neighbour, least of all a neighbour who would carry books and an ink-horn on a hurried and enforced journey.'

I said roughly: 'How may you know that my

journey is hurried and enforced?' And he smiled again.

'There are ways of telling. But let not that disturb you. In fact, to comfort you I may say that I am in the same boat. Indeed, possibly in just these circumstances was the byword coined, "in the same boat".'

'That,' I said gloomily, 'is most unlikely.' There was only one Richard Fairfax and only one Diana Bye – and only one wretched, unlucky Robert Younge, who had run the one through the body and left the other without so much as a word of farewell. I sat down on the comfortless bunk and stared before me.

'Why, be of better cheer, man,' said the stranger. 'What say the ancients? "To the past ill of action or of fortune add not the present ill of sorrow." You will think for a long time before you better that.' And so saying he turned and left me and almost at the same moment a tremor ran through every timber of the *Firebird* – our journey had begun.

And now upon my thoughts of regret and sorrow at parting a faint cheer stole. I had of all things feared the loneliness and the spiritual starvation that I had imagined would be a necessary evil of my exile. We who were young in those years after the Armada had indeed seen all things made new. New books born of old knowledge, new faith born of old creeds, and new paths carved out upon the old sea. And we were young together, Basil, Kenneth, Ralph, and I. We had seen the dawn whiten outside the windows while we read verses to one another, we had enjoyed all the pleasures of the discoverers as we dived into the depths of books and brought up for one another's delight such gems as 'Even such is time' or 'An expense of spirit in a waste of shame is lust in action.' I smile now, remembering that we who had delight in such verse were ignorant of the work of time, its power to destroy and heal; and yet more ignorant of the action of lust, so strong a power that the expense of the spirit seems at the moment less than a penny thrown to a beggar. Perhaps the words pleased us with their suggestion of a knowledge that we did not possess, and perhaps that is why poetry is read by the young and mocked by the old. Be that as it may, on this bright April morning, as the *Firebird* stood off the Norfolk coast on her way to Guinea, I was aware of a lightening of my heart; my neighbour had noticed my folios, had quoted aptly enough from the classics, and had confided in me – perhaps here was the substance from which a friendship might be moulded.

Now when I say that our friendship seemed to be pre-ordained, make not the mistake of thinking that I hold with Calvin and his crew; for I loathe that as a pernicious and unchristian doctrine. I mean rather that we were thrown together in a way that made either love or hatred inevitable between us. We two took our meals – sorry enough they were, too – with the Captain, who was a very silent man as a rule, but whether that silence covered great wisdom or only stupidity I never discovered. He had no mate, it seemed, and was a man with a rough tongue and ready fist, so that none of his crew loved him overmuch ... which was, later, very well for us. So at first Alan and I would begin our talks at the table and rise still talking, followed often enough by a scornful glance from the Captain; then we would wander on the deck or into one or another of our cabins, and the talk would grow more intimate and free.

I would inquire into the source of his learning, and he would tell me about his grandmother, who taught him first to read and write and cipher. She had been a nun, he said, who had consorted with gypsies and at last taken an ale-house within sight of the sea. She was, he said, a very able woman, no less handy with the distaff than with the quill, a woman of great beauty and many lovers. He would talk about her by the hour, telling tale after tale of her courage, her resourcefulness, her wisdom. Sometimes I teased him, for that was ever the way to draw from him a new and better story:

'One would think that your grandmother was the Phoenix,' I said once. And to that he replied:

'... I should sin
To think but nobly of my grandmother,
Good wombs have borne bad sons.'

And I foolishly let every word of Will's that he quoted forge a new link between us, and long before we reached Guinea I loved him for his knowledge and his wit. I told him, naturally, that I was in hiding, having killed the Queen's favourite in a duel, and what the duel was about. He laughed and said that one could tell the age of men by the kinds of duels they fought, as men could tell horses by their teeth. No man over the age of twenty-five ever challenged another about a woman. Why not? Because by that time they knew that nothing could be said about women or done to them that was worse than they deserved. I asked him if he did not like women; he replied that he adored them ... in their proper place – bed. I was embarrassed to realize that of that aspect of women I knew nothing, so I changed the subject by reminding him that he too was running away.

'From what?' I asked.

'Hanging,' he said, 'for killing a man.'

'Who?' I asked, and: 'How – why? Tell me all about it.'

'A man,' he said; 'it was in our ale-house. We were both drunk, and we quarrelled. That's all. We went outside to fight it out, and I killed him. I've got a horrible temper.'

'Are you sorry?' I asked.

'Sometimes. When I think that he'll never eat food or drink ale or lie with a woman again. I'd have been sorrier still, I suppose, if I'd been killed and so lost all these good things.'

Sometimes he shocked me by treating with levity

ideas that I had been reared to respect, and, as the weather grew warmer and tempers shorter, we quarrelled more than once. But he could always bring me round after an argument without making an effort to do so. One night when the cabins were too stifling hot for sleep, we lay on mats on the deck and watched the moon rise. The moon dragged our talk round to the goddess Diana and I told him a thing which I had hitherto withheld, the name of the woman who still filled all my thoughts.

'Mm,' he said, 'I've heard of her. Fairfax was right in what he said, you know. Nay, where's the sense in denying it? And if you call me out I shall take no notice. Face the truth, boy. Forget her. Once you've known a woman you'll realize that all the things men say about them must perforce be true. When we sail from Guinea, there'll be women on board. I vow that I'll pick you out the one that I would otherwise have picked for myself and . . .'

'A Negress,' I said, with disgust. 'Am I, who have seen Sydney's Stella and Will's Dark Lady, to consort with a greasy Negress, with filed teeth and dugs like empty sacks? Thank you, Alan Winfarthing, you can keep her for yourself.'

At this peevish speech he burst into a roar of laughter.

'Every Negress doesn't file her teeth, and they haven't all borne children. Can't you imagine a sleek little body of black ivory, with a head like a black lamb's back? And can't you imagine what they know . . . have you never heard the proverb: "Out of Africa comes every new thing"? You must live and learn, boy, or you'll never live.'

I confess that the phrase 'a head like a black lamb's back' did stir something deep in me, but I made no reply. I was angered at his attitude towards me. After all, he was only the grandson of a tavern-keeper, while I was heir to Longmere. I admitted him to my company because he was a scholar, but I was not going to have him dictating to me upon a question of morals. So I lay sulkily upon my mat until the eastern sky was flushed with the colour of the tea-roses that climbed around my window at home. As the thin light spread over the ship, I looked at him with new eyes, eyes that were going, I determined, to learn to hate him. I studied the swarthy lean face, in which his pale eyes shone with so startling a contrast, and the thin-lipped hard mouth above the little black peaked beard. I thought of the thousands of words that had fallen from those tight lips to gladden or to sear my heart, and I tried to harden myself against him. Then suddenly he rose and stood by the side.

'Awake, for morning with one spear of light
Has scattered all the forces of the night,'

he murmured. Straightway I forgot my resolves.

'What is that?' I cried. 'I have never heard it.'

'No; it is from the East. My father was a sailor of Venice; I once went a voyage with him. I heard that poem in its own language. One day perhaps I will turn it into English ... or perhaps not. It might lose something, like Cranmer's Bible.'

'At least, say it for me,' I begged. He laughed again and said:

'You might not approve, it is not a very pious poem, nor is its spirit quite that of the Church of England.' Alas for early training, I was more than ready to renounce all interest in the Church of England. And when Alan reached that final hopeless line, 'Turn down my unused glass,' I was well rewarded.

All this time we were drawing nearer to Guinea, and I hoped that Alan had forgotten his promise. At last we anchored and the boats went up a tributary of the great river, returning laden with miserable blacks closely shackled together. The Captain had firmly refused to let me go with the boats. He said that even the chief who sold him the slaves was not to be trusted, and that he had no wish to go back to my father with the story that I had had a poisoned arrow in my back. Alan went once, but no more; then he joined me in the shadow where I sat reading and said:

'I've never been slaving before, and I shan't come again.'

'Is the Captain pleased with the cargo?' I asked, for I knew that upon its value would the slaver's rather uncertain temper depend.

'I believe so. He's a swine. He's got more than he's got room for, Robert. Poor devils, they won't be able to breathe.'

'Can't we ask him not to?' I asked.

'Oh, Robert, there speaks the village squire. Markham wouldn't listen to God or the Devil, if it was a question of making a fourpenny profit. I did venture upon a slight protest and he told me to mind my – no, I won't repeat it, to mind my own business. And he doesn't know why *I* took ship with him, so I'm afraid he wouldn't listen to you.'

Nevertheless, at the evening meal I brought up the matter. Wrinkling my nose at the rancid odour of my salt pork I asked:

'Get a good cargo, Captain?'

'Ah, splendid, two hundred and ten, all able-bodied, and nearly all the women are young – an advantage that, eh, Mr. Winfarthing?' He leered at Alan, whom in his general good humour he had quickly forgiven.

'Two hundred and ten,' I repeated. 'Where are you putting that number?'

'In the hold, proper place. Like to see them?'

That I ignored. 'I can't see how you got that number in at all,' I persisted.

'Oh, easy enough, they're all laid out, head to head, and heel to heel, as neat as herring in a barrel.'

'Comfortable?' I asked, feeling peculiarly foolish. The Captain suddenly saw the drift of the conversation.

'That lousy milksop has been getting at you, has he? I suppose he thought if I wouldn't mind him I might you, you being Squire's son. We'll, we aren't in Longmere now, young man, and I shall pack my slaves where and how I like and not take any orders from runaway young murderers with the marks of the cradle still on their backsides. God strike me if I hadn't picked you out two of the neatest little wenches of the whole boiling, and I damned now if you shall so much as look at 'em.'

Much to my shame, I found myself growing more and more crimson in the face as his speech went on. I felt that Alan was looking at me with an 'I told you so' expression. I looked at him to see if this was so and found that he was staring hard at his plate, with no expression but that of disgust upon his face. I was sorry then that I had even twitted him, if only in my thoughts, with being of simple blood. Only a gentleman would have refrained just then from looking at me. The Captain, having lighted his pipe, as if he were waiting to see if either of us had anything else to say, strode away. Then Alan raised his eyes from his plate and smiled at me.

'He must respect you very deeply at heart,' he said. 'You should have heard how he described me.'

So the slaves were, I supposed to be kept like herring in a barrel. Before very long a peculiar sickly odour began to pervade the whole vessel. One fell asleep with it in one's nostrils and it was the first thing of which one became conscious upon waking. After a day or so, every morning saw a black body, sometimes two or three, go hurtling into the sea, and presently we had an escort of sharks, that appeared as punctually as dogs awaiting a meal of bones. This was not without its effect upon Alan, whose lazy cheery cynicism was shaken as I had never expected to see it. Once, when I had complained of the stench, he said: 'It's bad, but there's something worse, a kind of cloud of misery that darkens the very sun.'

'It seems so wasteful' I said; 'if they took fewer and troubled to keep them alive, they'd be just as well off in the end.'

'I pointed that out to him, that morning. No good. It's the excitement of seeing a lot cheap that goes to his head, as brandy does to mine, and drives out reason.'

Our lives were less pleasant in a sense, because of increasing friction with the Captain. He had not forgiven what he regarded as Alan's persistence and my impudence. He never missed an opportunity of being insolent or of dragging before us, always at mealtimes, some grisly detail about the condition of the slaves. He had a tiny young one in his cabin at times, he may even have had several, they were so much alike to me. At first neither Alan nor I took any notice of this, but as the days dragged on, the food grew worse, the wind slackened, and still the slaves died and died and died, his temper grew ever the more uncertain and sometimes we heard cries from the Captain's cabin – once, listening carefully, we caught the sound of blows. On that particular evening I was surprised on looking at Alan to see that his thin sneering lips were white, making a queer light line between his dark moustache and beard. 'One day I'm going to give him such a thrashing,' he said. I smiled and reminded him that he had once told me that women deserved all that was said of or done to them.

'Great God,' he said, without passion, 'I don't call these women in that sense. They're little more than animals, that's why I can't bear to see them suffer.'

There was pain in his voice, and I thought with relief that the first stopping-place, Trinidad, was near. We should unship some there, and the rest, having more room, would perhaps not die quite so readily and perhaps not smell so bad. But someone had been before us at Trinidad and we sold only fifty. From that time onwards the Captain grew more and more surly, and our one consolation was that we were not members of his crew. Directly we left Trinidad I fell sick. I lay in my bunk and shivered and shuddered, while Alan lapped me warmly and laid a hot brick to my back and another to my feet, and straightway I was hotter than St. Lawrence on his grid; then I pushed back the covers and was forthwith shuddering again. My mind wandered too, so that at times I was at home and saw the roses on the terrace and the deer between the beeches in the park. And once I held Diana in my arms. She wore a veil over her face and bosom, and at the touch of her warm flesh beneath my hands, all my manhood moved within me so that I tore the veil in order to kiss her lips and the white hollow of her neck where the little pulse beat. And it was not Diana under the veil, but a black woman. From dreams like that I would struggle up to find Alan holding a tankard to my lips or a wet clout to my head. At first I was rebellious and questioned whether it was for this that I had escaped from Dick Fairfax's sword and the Queen's anger, to die like a poisoned rat in a hole. Then at length, what with my weakness, the dreams, and the aching in my bones, I began to long for death and went back to the teaching of my childhood, and began to hope that paradise would be a little like my Longmere woods. So I continued, while the *Firebird* stopped at Haiti and left thirty slaves behind and then drew on towards Cuba. Alan went ashore at Cuba and came back with some greyish powder lapped in a piece of palm leaf. He mixed some of this in a pannikin of water and supported my head while I drained it. It was a very bitter potion, which left the skin of my mouth rough and dry, but within the half-hour I was sweating so that my blankets were wet like Gideon's fleece and the pain had gone from my bones. Moreover, my stomach was crying out for the solidity of ship's biscuit and a great slice of cheese. When I had eaten, and tested my legs, which were exceeding weak, I fell into a natural slumber. From this dreamless bliss I was awakened by the sound of voices raised in anger and then a noise as of blows. There was silence again almost immediately and I was dozing once more, when the door opened and Alan stepped over the sill. His mouth was bleeding and one eye was closed in a great swelling. Still his eyes and the uninjured side of his mouth were smiling.

'Well, are you better?' I nodded. 'I hope we didn't disturb you.'

'It's gone,' I said, joyfully. 'I'm hungry again. Tell me what the row was about.'

'Are you feeling stronger? If not I won't tell you now.'

'Never better, except for my knees.'

'Well then, Robert, I've just killed the Captain.'

'You can't have,' I said. 'I know what's wrong with you, you've caught my fever and you've had one of those dreams I was telling you about.'

'No, my boy. I'm in my right mind ... and he's dead. We had another row and I hit him. Then we had a fight and the chance came to me to kill him and I did, deliberately. I always did hate him, and when I'm angered I do want to kill people. So I did. Oh dear, he's the second this year too.' Alan sat down on the foot of my bunk, wearing such a comic expression of dismay that I laughed as loudly as my weakness would allow.

'Well, I can't let the men know till I've seen how the land lies. I'll say he's sick like you and that I'm looking after him. We're supposed to be making for Vera Cruz with the rest of the blacks. Great God, there's no mate! Suppose I've killed the one man who could navigate this old Ark.'

He went lounging away, but I called him back.

'You can't go with a face like that, they'd all know at once. I'll go.'

So, fighting against the great waves of dizziness that swept against me as I moved, I got myself on deck, told my story and found a man who was quite able, he said, to take us into the harbour at Vera Cruz, supposing that the Captain's illness would be as persistent as mine. I added that we would look after the Captain and that no one else had better come near for fear of infection. I went back to Alan, feeling that I had made a success of my errand.

'All you must do now is to see that Wright is obeyed,' I said.

'That'll be easy,' said Alan; 'now I'll show you what all the row was about.' He threw open his cabin door, and stood aside so that I might look in. For a moment I saw nothing, partly because I did not know what to look for as a visible cause of a quarrel, and partly because the person concerned was sitting perfectly still in a little heap on the floor. It was a little West Indian girl, beautiful with the dainty, evanescent beauty of immaturity. She was of a rather deep but very even brown colour and had very black shiny hair, pushed back behind her ears and falling on to her shoulders. Except for a wreath of leaves and flowers, rather broken and withered, that fell down over her tiny pointed breasts, she was naked to the waist; here she wore a belt of woven grass from which a thick fringe of loose grasses fell out in a frill over her legs and around her as she sat on the floor. She sat up very straight and her still eyes and hands gave her the appearance of a little bronze statue, like some I have seen in churches.

Alan broke in on my appreciative silence:

'A beauty, isn't she? Far too good to go cutting sugar-cane, or waiting in the market for some gross old man in search of a titbit.'

'You bought her? What was the row about?'

'Oh, Markham said he wouldn't have her on board. That pricked me, especially after the scurvy way he served us over his black beauties. I said that I was a passenger and if I'd bought an ape or a dog or a parrot I would have been allowed to bring it on board; so I twitted him with jealousy. And so we went on. That's all. He said some vile things and so did I. I don't suppose even a good-tempered man likes having his concupiscence exactly reckoned and described. Besides, who would like to send her ashore, having seen her? Come here.'

The last words were addressed to the girl, who did not understand them of course; but she smiled at the accompanying gesture, rose up from her frill of grass, and came forward with a mixture of shyness and boldness to take the hand that Alan held out to her.

I was suddenly and unreasonably jealous. Doubly jealous. I was going to lose Alan. There would be no more long exciting talks, lying on the deck under the stars. He would be below in the darkness, wrapped in those thin brown arms. An envy of something that I had never known shot through me, and all these feelings were oddly mixed with thoughts of Diana and memories of things I'd read.

'I'm going to lie down,' I said shortly. Alan took me by the elbow.

'You are recovered?' he asked. And I remembered that he had tended me and even in the excitement of his purchase had thought to buy me the potion that had, I felt, saved my life.

'Thanks to you, yes,' I mumbled. 'Good night.' I lay for a little, torturing myself with the idea of what was going on in the next cabin. For what orgy had my removal been the signal to begin? Finally I made up my mind that at Vera Cruz I myself would go ashore and do some shopping.

Next day brought me new strength and I went around with Alan as he and the sailor Wright between them attended to the Captain's duties. It was a hot cloudless day, and, although I had enjoyed many such since I had left England in a downpour of April rain, today I felt all the joy of a prisoner newly released. Presently Alan drew me aside.

'Unpleasant duty awaits me,' he said. 'The Captain

is still lying upon his bunk. I fear that the weather is too hot for this storage. I must get him ready for putting overboard at some convenient moment.' I gave a little shudder. And because I was ashamed of my thoughts overnight and of that shudder, I said: 'Let me come with you, I can lend a hand.' He looked at me oddly.

'Ever see a dead man, Robert?'

'Not closely, but it's a chance to begin.'

'That's the spirit. Come on, then.'

Despite my words I knew a tremor of the stomach as Alan threw open the Captain's door. I saw once more in a moment of time all the countless occasions on which I had seen that burly bowlegged figure go through that door, on some of them to be greeted by the little waiting Negress.

There was already a still and horrible flavour about that cabin. I wondered how Alan could go in in such a cool and businesslike way. I imagined how I should have felt if the day after the duel I had been required to dispose of Dick Fairfax's body; I remembered old stories of suspected murderers who broke down when confronted with the bodies of their victims. But Alan went straight to the bunk and began winding the still and bulky figure in a length of tarpaulin.

'What happened to him exactly?' I asked.

'Went over and broke his neck, I think. I didn't really find out. He fell heavy; these fat men do.' Very deftly he went on with his work. I realized that what makes lying out such slow work as a rule is the fact that the workers handle the corpse as if its feelings had been rendered doubly sensitive by death. Alan might have been folding up a heavy bundle of sacks. 'Callous,' I thought, 'lustful and bloody and callous.' I realized too that our spiritual companionship had ended on the previous night, not when he told me of the Captain's death, but when he showed me the case of the quarrel.

'And now I think that the way to rouse least

suspicion will be to announce his death, and publicly commit him to the deep. He might have come to a better end, or worse. Anyway, I've done my best with tarpaulin and roundshot to lay him as a sailor should. Tomorrow all the blackamoors are going to be soused down and brought up for a sniff of God's good air. And then ... what in the Devil's name, Robert, am I going to do with them? Shall I water at Vera Cruz and then take them back to Guinea?'

'Why not sell them there? If you take them back they'll die on the way or get taken prisoner again the moment they get back.' I am afraid that my ideas of the rights and wrongs of slave-trading were those of the ordinary person, not a person like Alan, who could kill a man as he would a fly that annoyed him and yet who was now glowering at me for making a perfectly ordinary suggestion.

'I'm surprised at you, Robert.' That was all he said, but with such disdain in his voice that I minded me once more of the tavern and the broad acres of Longmere. I went away offended and I saw him no more that day, for he took his new duties seriously, though I do not believe that he knew anything about navigation.

Once more I went to bed, tantalized by the sight as I passed his door of the girl whom he called Kalula combing her black hair with Alan's comb; once more I soothed myself with the promise that I would buy myself a flower-wreathed beauty and perhaps, having more money, an even lovelier one than Kalula. My last thought was that if on the morrow the question of slaves came up again, I would tell him that he did worse than sell slaves, since if there was no market there would be no slaves, and that he had become part of that market.

I was very deeply asleep when I felt a hand take my

shoulder, and shake me with increasing violence. When my eyes, which had been weak in my fever, had ungummed themselves, I could scarcely see Alan's face above me, for my cabin was full of bellying smoke-clouds.

'Get up. Don't dress; grab your things and your money, then go up, get into the boat – they're lowering them now – take Kalula, and if you get through, stand by her. I meant to marry her. The Great Harry, Welland, to my grandmother. You understand?'

All this he said in a quick, yet perfectly controlled voice, so clearly spoken that I have, after all these years repeated it word for word. I remember that I cried:

'And you?'

But, his orders given, he had gone and in his place stood Kalula, a blanket over her shoulders, crying and clutching my arm and jabbering to me in some unknown tongue. How he had made her comprehend that she was to come with me I could not understand, but in all the haste of that awful moment he had managed to do so.

Above all was confusion, although it was clearer there, for the smoke that poured out had all the world to lose itself in. The fire had gained a tremendous hold; I believe that in the supposed illness of the Captain, and with Alan below with his charmer, every soul upon the *Firebird* had been asleep.

One of the men cried out to me: 'Room here, Master Robert,' and when Kalula and I had scrambled into place the boat was full and was pushed off. It was like a moment in a dream, full of unsavoured excitement. I did not think that there was the *Firebird* burning, and here were we who had entrusted our lives to her keeping launched out on the sea in open boats. I only saw the smoke, shot now with flames, rolling up to the paling stars, and nearer the men in the boats bearing the curious things that they had snatched up to bring with them and clad in the first clothes that came to hand.

I was not fully clad myself, so I dressed as well as I could and then went on watching the *Firebird* and wondering about Alan. I have never seen anything burn so rapidly; the sun that had shone upon us for weeks had dried all the timbers and canvas, so that they were a very food for the flames. We had already put some distance between us and the ship, because the men said, which I did not realize before, that if the ship went down and we were near, we might be drawn in too. And now, looking back, we saw the ship all outlined with light, and then, like a scene in hell, a pattern of dark forms appeared against the light. They were all naked, except one, whose pattern showed up distinct from the others. That I knew was Alan. The dancing black forms were not, it appeared, engaged in senseless activity; now one and now another would appear with a barrel or a plank and Alan was lashing them on to these and throwing them overboard. But the supply of loose timber gave out before the last slave had gone over, and the remainder stood for a second in a ragged black fringe on the edge of the burning ship; then they dived together. Alan must have been among this remnant; for when next I looked back, there were no figures dancing among the flames.

Then I said – and my voice when I spoke was the voice of my father when he speaks to be obeyed – 'Sucking under or no sucking under, we are rowing back to pick him up.' There were a few demurs, a few half-hearted protests at the folly of risking more lives for the sake of black trash that the sharks would eat anyhow. But an old gruff sailor shouted that it was a brave deed, and it was up to them to be as good men as he. And back we went. The surface was broken by bobbing black heads, and some near us raised pleading hands and faces. But the faces were black, we were looking for a white one . . . which we did not find. There were, we knew, sharks in the water, and now and then the black heads went down, screaming. I wondered whether this change in the way they died was worth Alan's sacrifice. I could almost hear his cool, unemphatic voice say: 'I only wanted to give the poor devils the same chance as I had.' And the same death, Alan. For though we searched till morning, we did not find him. And ever since, in the struggles that we made to exist in the next days, in my eventual happy homecoming, in the delivery of Kalula, great with child, to the incredibly old grandmother at the Great Harry, in all my life since, in my marriage and my joy in my children, I have been conscious of a core of sorrow too deep to influence my outer self. I think of how we parted that morning by the Captain's body, I think of his narrow brown face and his eyes, I think of his verses and those he might have written, and man that I am now, the unshed tears run salt down my throat like blood from an inner wound. Sometimes in church I am assured that after life there is death and after death a more enduring life in a happier world, and then I hope for it, if only to see Alan again. But I remember that he scoffed at the idea of the life everlasting. He would believe that he ended in that fire-lighted sea; or if he endured at all, that it is in the little brown-faced light-eyed boy who, at my request, bears his name at the Great Harry.

SERGEANT SALATHIEL CHRIST-WITH-US ROPER BEGINS A LETTER TO HIS FRIEND

A.D. 1651

CHAPTER THREE

ICONOCLASTS

To my friend and fellow-worker in God, greeting. You bade me let you know how we fared and, as the Captain in charge hath tonight divers papers to dispatch to my Lord, the time seemeth opportune for the sending of this poor screed to you. The work proceeds apace; and if I say that oftentimes the sight of the destruction that is inseparable from the cause giveth me pain, you will understand that it is not because I favour the idolatrous and ungodly images, windows, and such baubles, but rather because I grieve that the Devil hath entrenched himself so firmly behind that which is pleasing to the eye. In this district there have been closed one hundred and four alehouses – and, except in the case of which more hereafter, with but little opposition and no bloodshed. At the great church at Welland were found divers Popish vestments, prick-song books and a Book of Common Prayer. All of these were destroyed with great zeal. At Cawley a Babylonish font, after the troopers had defiled the waters thereof, was used to baptize their horses. I am not, however, of the opinion that the work is put forward by such measures, which savour to me of the old mummery nevertheless some are of the opinion that play of this kind offers the men encouragement and thereby strengthens their zeal.

At Welland we met opposition from a strange quarter. There we found an ale-house cunningly placed by the sea and away from the highroad. A sign over the door, which was at once cut down together with a great part of the thatch, bore the effigy of King Henry VIII. A body of us went within to empty the barrels and break down the copper in which the Devil's brew is made. Men for this work have, as you know, to be chosen with discretion; for many a one having put his hand to the plough hath looked backward, to be like Lot's wife confounded. Within were but three people, an old woman of an alien race, wearing an immodest gown of scarlet cloth, a man whom we took for her son, and a young girl. Yet did these three bolt and lock the door of the cellar and refuse to give up the key. Then the Captain, like the thunderbolt of Jehovah that he is, gave order to bind the people and break down the door of the cellar by force. This was done and within was found, not ale only, but divers other liquors of which Scripture saith: 'Wine is a mocker, strong drink is raging.' All these were emptied out save only the brandy, which the Captain bade spare, it being a great virtue in sickness, and therewith had set aside to take to his lodging, where he keepeth sundry simples and medicines for the relief of sickness. At that the man calls out: 'I have seen robbers of many kinds and colours, but never before have I seen those that rob do it in the name of God.' Upon this the Captain says that unless he stills his tongue it shall be tied for him. 'As you will,' says the man, 'I would as soon be gagged with a piece of filthy cloth as with ill-quoted Scripture texts, and the good liquor like Abel's blood crying from the ground.' At this evidence of stiffneckedness the Captain begins to look around for some reason for offence, for here doubtless was an enemy that should be destroyed, root and branch. And there upon the wall was one of those images of Mary, the like of which I should not have thought would have been in England since the Queen left. There were flowers on a ledge before it. We had stumbled by chance upon one of Baal's strongholds. The Captain, with his sword, cuts off the plaster head and scatters the flowers, whereat the old woman gives a great cry, and said that it belonged to the holy woman who was dead. Much else she said, but her speech was broken. And the man began to struggle with the trooper who was holding him.

'I care nothing for the image,' he shouted, 'but that you should come into a private place to give rein to your whim – why, Charles himself, whom you dogs called tyrant, would have knocked on the door and doffed his hat to the lady of the house.' And he indicated the snuffling old coloured woman, who was still muttering about a holy woman. And I saw our Captain signal with his eyes to the man who was holding the tavern-keeper, and he took him by the throat as if to shake him into silence, but he bent back his head. And there was a deep silence in the kitchen. The girl began to cry: 'You have killed him.'

'It is not killing, to destroy the enemies of the Lord. Read the story of Samuel and Agag, else. And ye who remain had better look to your ways.' And with that we came out of the tavern, for the Captain's voice was final. One man after another added his word – 'Even so perish all Thine enemies, Lord,' and other such. For a moment I regretted the death of one who, meseemed, was a brave man. Think not from this, my friend, that I waver in the good work ... but hadst thou seen him, speaking his mind freely, in the face of us all.

Methinks that overmuch of my time hath been devoured by this account of an affair of little moment; you will wish to know more of the revelation of faith....

A JACOBITE TELLS THE STORY OF AN ARCTIC INTERLUDE A.D. 1747

CHAPTER FOUR

ARCTIC INTERLUDE

YESTERDAY I suddenly realized what it is to be old. A boy went past my window humming a tune; for hours afterwards I tried to remember where I had heard it before and what words were set to it; the effort to remember dredged up a host of half-forgotten things, but that song was not amongst them. Then as I was falling asleep the song, its words, its singer, and the scene in which I heard it first, came into my drowsy mind clearly and yet remotely, as a distant scene will come to view when the glass focuses it. Then I realized that I was old indeed to have forgotten such a thing. Today it is all so real and vivid to me that I seem to smell the smoke that used to go up from the vats, dragging curtains of gloom over the pale sky. But for how long shall I hold it so securely in my mind? For indeed the mind of the old is like a cupboard whose pegs have rotted, and the happenings of the years lie muddled as the clothes would on the floor of such closet.

In the summers of 1746 and 1747 I was with the whalers of Leisburg. The very ruins of that wooden town have vanished now; it was tumbling to decay as the last sail left its harbour, following its wealthier rival, Smeerenberg, into the region of lost cities. But when I knew it first, it was a flourishing place, with inns and shops and drinking-saloons and brothels and even a church where a few of the more seriously minded of the Dutch Protestants went occasionally before a specially dangerous trip, or after a specially profitable one. It was of course only a summer colony; I think that I am right in saying that no one had, at that time, ever spent a winter so far north. They were afraid, not only of the cold and hunger, for they were combatable evils, but of the more subtle terrors of the dark silent loneliness.

Women followed the whalers as the men followed the whales, for gold; and the men, reeking of blood and blubber and alcohol, threw gold or gold's equal into the frowsy laps in which they lolled. Many of these women were the dregs of the European ports, camp-followers in this new and profitable campaign; many no doubt were honest women, sharing their men's hardships, if not their dangers, in a way that would have been impossible before such settled bases as Leisburg were established. Honest or not, pretty or repulsive they were alike lacking in interest for me. Exiled after the disasters of '45, my lands forfeit and a rather flattering price upon my head, I was in little mood for dalliance, gentle or otherwise.

Then one evening I saw a woman go into a drinking place and brothel known as Jake's. A very popular establishment it was, for its owner was content with no more than about one hundred and fifty per cent profit and had been known to sell an egg for a shilling when it could not be obtained elsewhere in the place for less than twenty pence. I did not notice much about the woman, except that she was tall and walked with a certain pride and had black hair, closely braided over her crown, and wore a white cloak. I do not believe people who say that at the first casual meeting they notice the colour of a stranger's eyes or every feature of his face. I mentioned the woman to a man named Duncan, who sailed with me and was a notorious gossip and busybody, often a valued source of information. Valuable, that is to say, when one had learned to leaven one's credulity with a certain amount of scepticism. However, I approached him, hopefully now, and was not disappointed. 'Oh, so someone's caught your eye at last? And you're just too late. She's the pick of the basket and your choice is a credit to one so young; but Holtzen's got her, and she ain't looking elsewhere this season. Know her name? Why, I know the name, and a lot besides that about every living soul in this town. Name's Jane Winfarthing, and she came out here with her father. He used to go drunk on duty and was drowned, naturally. Now I hear that she's leaving with Holtzen tomorrow or next day. But he don't care for thin wenches as a rule, which is odd his choosing her. Still, if she eats at his table she'll soon suit his taste fine. Anything else you'd care to know?'

'No, thanks.'

'I'm sorry your luck was so dead out. Have to be quicker another time.'

'I'll remember your sound advice.'

Two days later Holtzen sailed, and the woman went with him. The summer passed and the motley colony emptied; the whalers and storekeepers and the women went southwards and Leisburg settled down for a winter's sleep. Once or twice during the winter I caught myself remembering the black hair and the free walk of the woman who had sailed with fat old Holtzen, and I hoped that he had forgotten his prejudice against thin women and perhaps even married her. I thought of her, when I did so, in a brightly painted house, with a poplar-shaded road running past it, and a field of hyacinths by the side. I hoped that Holtzen had had better luck than we had. I had not even made enough to take me to France, the place that was at that moment both the refuge and Mecca of all Jacobite youth. Instead I went herring-fishing off Newfoundland and learned to mend a net, to caulk a seam, and to eschew political argument. Then the spring came again, and with the lengthening days we turned our faces to the north. Leisburg was already full of faces strange and familiar, and loud as Babel with the clacking of Dutch and English, Scotch and Scandinavian tongues. And all the tongues were wagging upon one string. Something that they regarded as a miracle had arrested the whaler's attention. Seven people, we learned, had been picked up by a northward-bound boat after spending the whole winter in the Arctic darkness. They were suffering somewhat from hunger and frostbite, but they were all sane and cheerful. Such a thing had never been known before.

Duncan was, as usual, the first with the news. He came back with information simply bubbling out of him.

'Holtzen's boat it was, cracked to bits in the ice, and him drowned; and these walked until they found a bit of an island. And I'm forgetting the thing I've run half a mile to tell you: one of the seven is that woman, you remember; the one you asked about last year. You should hear the men talk about her; guardian angels ain't in it with her, according to them. She's back up at Jake's, and he making a fortune with the crowd that there is to see her. Why don't you go along?'

Most unnecessary question, for I was going even as he asked it, and I went so quickly that I did not ask myself what I expected to see or do when I got there. I only recalled and dwelt on the sight of her calm face and upright figure as she passed me once in the squalid street.

Jake's was full to the door, and the atmosphere, to one coming in from the clear night air, was like a blow in the face. Clouds of tobacco-smoke had drifted to the low ceiling and, unable to find any escape, hung there like fog. The dampness of condensed breath ran in streams down the wooden walls, and the reek of unwashed bodies mingled with the sharper scents of gin and brandy. As I entered, a man slipped helplessly drunk from a wooden stool near the door, and I sat down on it promptly. I ordered brandy for myself, and, my eyes accustoming themselves to the glare of light and the fog of smoke, I looked around. She was sitting at the end of the room in a niche among a stack of barrels and she was already extremely drunk. As my eyes lit on her she threw back her head and laughed, and the light caught her fringe of white teeth and the dark cavern of her throat. Then she lifted the tankard that she held and drank deeply. Next, leaning forward, she whispered something into the ear of one of the men near her, and he repeated it to his neighbour and he to his until the whole crowd was laughing at what was evidently a joke. In the midst of their laughter the woman fell as suddenly serious and looked round her with the blind narrow stare of intoxication. Not till then did I notice her eyes, clear and icy as water, with the pupils mere pin-points like the black dots in frogs' spawn. 'Pitch us a song, Jane,' someone cried, and the rest took it up.

'One of the old ones,' called out a man with his arm in a rough canvas sling.

'You must be sick to death of hearing them, and I don't know any new ones. My ballad-monger hasn't called very regularly just lately.'

Renewed laughter greeted this sally.

'Give us "The Month of May,"' cried the man with his arm in the sling.

I had been disappointed in her voice when she spoke, though why I should use the word 'disappointed' I don't know; why should every word that she said in that raucous screaming tone have fallen like sharp stones on my ears? But when, without setting down her tankard or moving in any way from her lolling position, she began to sing, I was enchanted. It was not a sweet voice, but it was strong and true and had in it the deep throb of distant drumming. And that was where and how I first heard the song that I could not remember yesterday:

'When in the pleasant month of May
If you should go a-wooing,

The maid will hardly say you nay
And may prove your undoing.

For what you sow in some dark spot
With much delight and laughter,
Ere spring returns may raise a crop
That comes to light hereafter.'

It was quite obviously a well-known song, for they tapped out the time with bottles and pipes and boot-heels; and yet they made her sing it over and over again, like children with a familiar story.

'Sang to 'em, she did,' said the man on the floor beside me in a thick dreamy voice; 'all through the night, when morning never came, and the ice groaned all around; she sang to 'em.' He rolled over and fell asleep on his back. The singing and the drinking went on until her voice began to catch and stumble; and her hair broke loose and fell on to her shoulders. Once, between two songs in which they all joined, I saw her put her hands on either side a man's head and kiss him soundly on both cheeks. Presently her dress slipped from her shoulders and showed her white flesh against the blackness of her hair.

And I watched the whole with horrified, hungry eyes, as one presses an aching tooth with the tongue. I had known her for what she was, but I had invested her with dignity and beauty, and both were torn away, thrown off for the amusement of a crowd of drunken ruffians. Sickened I stayed to the end. As suddenly as she did everything, she gathered her dress about her with some remnant of her old grace and tried to stand up. But she stumbled and fell forward into the arms of the man to whom she had whispered. They came swaying together down the length of the room. At the end of the counter she made another effort to stand and, by holding the dripping-board with one hand, managed to pull herself upright. He kept his hands on her though and made an attempt to lift her, but she shook him off. He protested, and she pushed herself free, saying in a loud voice:

'Let me alone. I've never had to be carried into bed yet, have I, boys?'

They read the true meaning into the question and laughed and shouted in reply. Someone suggested one more song.

'Not tonight. I'm tired. 'Night everybody.' She smiled round with blind and undiscriminating amiability and then went quickly round the end of the counter and through a door behind it. We all heard the bolt shoot home. The man beside me seemed to awake, yet he must have heard her last words, for he mumbled:

'Ay, tired I'll lay, poor wench; and sick of the sight of men.' I felt that there was no evidence of such sickness in her behaviour; but I said nothing, only opened the door and came away. It was six weeks before I visited Jake's again.

It was plain at the end of the first of those weeks that Leisburg as a whaling centre was doomed. Either the Leviathans had in some way learned that destruction awaited them there, or else the slaughter of past years had really cleared the seas around. Captain after captain returned with stories of disappointment and then turned eastward, with curses, never to sail into that harbour again. Coming back at the end of six weeks was like visiting a town where the plague had been just before.

Jake's was empty when I went in next time, and Jake with a long face was nailing down some chests, as if he too might leave at any moment.

'Trade slow?' I asked, as I gave my usual order.

'Slow, it's dead – both ends of it,' he added; and I understood that neither of his stores for the supply of men's pleasures was doing well.

'Last time I was here you were full to the doors; a woman called Jane was entertaining several friends.

What happened to her?' I tried to make my question the natural reply to his complaint.

'Back there,' he said with a jerk of the head. Then his face lightened. 'Care to see her?'

'I don't know,' I said.

'Don't you like the look of her?'

'Sometimes, not at others.' Never would I admit that I had seen her but twice.

'Well, of course if you're particular,' he sighed. 'Still, I was only trying to do her a good turn. Times are hard for her as well as me. And I can't raise the heart to turn her out, not after all them fellows said about her. Still, that don't buy victuals and she didn't save me, whatever she did for them.'

'She sang to them, didn't she?' It was a sneering question, and one I regretted afterwards. Jake spat.

'Sang to them be damned. Use your eyes on her, man, not your lugs.'

'Perhaps I will,' I said. 'I'll come round this evening.'

When finally the door behind the counter yielded to my hand, I would have given much to have been a mile from the place. I cursed the curiosity that had brought me there and the nervousness that assailed me now that I had come. She stood on the other side of a little table, and her hands were raised to pin up a loop of hair. The table was set for supper, and one candle stuck in a bottle-neck shed a circle of warm yellow light into the greyness of the Arctic evening. Her face was set in the lines of calmness that I had noticed at first, and when she spoke to me I was surprised again because her voice was like velvet, warm and soft.

'Good evening,' she said, and added the question with which one greeted everyone, friend and stranger, in Leisberg: 'And what was your luck?'

'Indifferent,' I said.

She motioned me towards the bed and sat down herself on the one stool that the room contained.

'You will wait while I eat perhaps? It is my first meal today.'

And then, before I could answer, she added: 'But you are also my first visitor; so if you choose not to wait . . .' She spread her hands palm-upwards in a little gesture of resignation that suddenly made me greatly ashamed.

I looked at the lump of greyish bread and the pieces of sodden salt fish that was all the table offered.

'Eat by all means,' I said, 'though that looks somewhat meagre to be breakfast, dinner, and supper.'

'It would have been more meagre still if you had not told Jake that you would come in tonight. He thought you might be good for half a guinea, so I got a shilling's-worth of food. It's a good shilling's-worth too.'

She pursed her lips and regarded her mean fare with a calculating yet hungry eye.

'But it's most inhospitable of me . . . won't you share the meal that the very sight of you provided?'

'If you will allow me to supplement it from the store.'

'As you wish,' she said without interest, and then as I reached the door she called after me:

'Don't bring any of the pickled cabbage. It looks all right, but a man sneezed all over it yesterday.'

I went carefully around the store and returned with a bottle of wine for which I paid roughly four times its value, a pat of salt but delicious butter, and a lump of Dutch cheese. Bad times were making Jake stingy. I longed to point out to him that, having met a bad season while he was provisioned for a good, his wisest course would be to sell his stuff cheaply and clear his store but that would have led to argument, and the woman was hungry and waiting, so I hurried back. During my absence she had halved her supper; the bread-plate with its portions of bread and fish stood at the place intended for me, while the fish-plate stood before her. I laid beside her the greater portion of my bread.

'I have eaten,' I said. I opened the wine, poured it into the thin horn glasses, and raised mine.

'To our better acquaintance,' I said.

She lifted hers: 'Amen to that,' and then fell upon her food with the eagerness engendered by a long fast. I noticed her hands for the first time; they were narrow and clean, precise and neat in their movements, while her manner of eating at an uncovered board, with the candle-grease running into a puddle at the foot of the bottle, was as fine as any I had ever seen. And she began, when the first few mouthfuls had taken the edge from her hunger, to make conversation as though she was indeed my hostess.

'You are whaling, of course?'

I nodded.

'With the Scots?'

'No; with the New Englander, Christy.'

'Do you like it?'

'I loathe it!'

'Then why?'

For some reason that I could not understand, I told her the truth.

'I've backed the wrong king rather heavily and had to leave my country in a hurry.'

'You are a Jacobite?'

Again I nodded.

She leaned forward and took the half-empty bottle in her hand to refill the glasses, then rose to her feet in a smooth unhurried movement that should have been accompanied by the rustling of silken skirts, and passed her glass over the pitcher of water that had been provided with her supper.

'The King,' she said.

I drank the toast and we sat down. It was a gesture that went to my heart, but it did more, it set me wondering. Where had she picked it up, the little secret movement that some of George's own Guards made over the fingerbowls of the mess-table? And then I was suddenly glad and proud that all those months ago I had distinguished her from the rest, that even the sight of the drunken orgy six weeks before had not entirely quenched my interest.

'Where do you come from? I asked.

'Welland, in Norfolk County. There's an inn there, only a stone's throw from the sea. It's shut now; my father fell foul of the Revenue men, so we shut it and came away. Then he was drowned, you know; so it's mine and I shall go back to it – if . . .'

'If what?'

'If I can get anyone to take me. I had great hopes of paying my way, but there isn't long now and no one about. I'll have to get someone to take me; meat for manners, you know. Only they all get rather Puritan once they turn southward and wifeward.'

It was a mere statement of fact and there was no rancour in her voice. She wetted a finger and gathered up one or two stray crumbs. Discomfort shot through me; the meal, a mere preliminary in any case, was over, and I had been aware almost since its beginning that my interest in her body had given place to an absorbing curiosity about her personality. I twisted the conversation round to the subject of her recent adventure.

'You should find no difficulty in getting a passage. You are the heroine of the whole settlement.'

She laughed in my face.

'Say "were"; for a couple of evenings, six weeks ago – and six weeks is a long time in a place where the year is only four months long. Oh, I'm not decrying the six of them, they'd help me if they could, but they're only before the mast themselves, and all scattered about on different boats now. They can't do much.'

'They praise you. That may interest someone. It interested me.'

'Did it? Why?'

'They say that you saved them, and I'm anxious to know how.'

'I didn't. If they say that, it is only the extravagance of gratitude.'

'For what?'

'Well, you know what common men are. They'll follow anyone blindly; a thing that has been done by someone else they'll do quite bravely, without knowing that they are being brave. But a thing that no one has done before terrifies them. I just wasn't frightened. My father wouldn't have been, nor would Holtzen; they were not common men. I wasn't frightened, because I knew all the time inside myself, somehow, that we'd live to get off; that I'd see my Great Harry again, the salty logs burning blue on the hearth and and the spit turning. Sometimes they doubted, but after the seal it was easier to make them believe me.'

'What seal?'

'The seal we caught. This really is interesting. We were hungry, you understand, and in need of fresh food. We saw seals and they shot one. It sank at once, just like a stone. The same thing happened three times; you wouldn't believe the effect that had on their minds. They were hungry, remember, and had so little powder and they were so superstitious. They said it wasn't natural, things shouldn't sink like that in salt water. They began to talk about the Devil, and when sailors do that they're heading for panic. I thought hard about it for days, and then, quite suddenly, I knew. Water like that isn't salt at the top. I drank some. I don't believe that anyone else knows that; people might even say I was lying or mad, but water like that isn't salt at the top. The ice melts or a river runs in under the ice or else the water is just different . . . and yet down below it is salt . . . well, I don't understand it, I only found out. So we started lasso practice. We lassoed one another. There's another thing. You think, and so does everyone else, that it is a time of unchanging night; but it isn't. There were always moments when we could see out of doors; so we practised, and the next seal we lassoed. I don't mean the very next – we missed often, but that was just bad luck; they didn't think that that was Satan; and after that we caught them. It was then they began to believe me when I said that we'd come through alive. I think that is all.'

'I see. And you sang, too, to cheer them?'

She looked at me hard for a moment, as if weighing her next words. Then she said, slowly:

'We all sang; it warmed us. But anyone can sing. If beyond having faith I did anything to save them from despair, it wasn't singing. There was one thing that only I could do, and that was to carry on the trade that I'd begun here in Leisburg.' She looked at me again with a slight rather tired smile that curved without parting her lips. I had forgotten that about her, forgotten that I myself had come there on no very noble errand. Her talk and the pictures it had called to my mind had blotted out the fact that she was talking to me as a shopkeeper entertains a customer, that I was sitting on a bed that anyone for a few shillings, might lie upon with her. I stared at her clear sea-water eyes, the neat black braids of her hair and the soft young body that she held so cheaply, and I thought of the six hairy, skinny, dirty scarecrows having their pleasure in it. I believe she saw my shudder.

'How strange you are!' she said. 'You knew what I was, and yet you are disgusted. Why? Have you yet to learn that it is only the carnal-minded who are so careful of their flesh? They know deep in themselves that they have nothing else.... They were so miserable, never warm enough, never quite not hungry; they'd seen their ship crushed like an eggshell, and Holtzen and their comrades drowned; they were like unhappy children. Yet you shudder at me because I tell you that

I gave them what I would have sold them here in this room a few days before ... what you yourself came here tonight to buy.'

'I know,' I said. 'That shudder deserves all the scorn that you can pour upon me. But indeed I had forgotten even why I came. Perhaps it wasn't even the usual thing that brings men here. Last year I saw you, just before you left with Holtzen. I saw you again just after you returned here. I wanted to see you again, to see what you are really.'

'No one knows what one is, or what anyone else is. Circumstances decide. There is a cannibal in every one of us, and a king too. Hunger will make us one, and honour the other. You have a great deal yet to learn.'

'That is true. And I have begun tonight. I am going now; but in gratitude for your conversation and because I owe you for a lesson, will you let me pay what you owe Jake and make sure that you will have at least two meals a day until you find a captain who is going south?'

'You are kind and I am grateful, but you are still not thinking clearly. You say you had forgotten what I am; we have talked, you have told me why you are here, we drank a certain toast together. For a little while we have been equals. Don't spoil it. Either we are two people, exiled, who have met by chance and broken bread together and so parted; or else we are bartering in a market and my part of the bargain is yet to be fulfilled. In one case you must not pay, in the other you must. Which is it to be?'

Something in me cried out to her – it was not desire, not even lust. She was beautiful there before my eyes, and her flesh was warm and fine. But the flesh, as she had said, was nothing; the glimpse that she had given me of her spirit had blinded me to her temporary lodging of blood and bone. If I could have mingled myself in some strange way with her spirit so that her gallantry and wisdom and courage might have had part in me for ever, how gladly would I have paid any price. But I could only think of the few poor coins in my pocket and stammer out something of a flash of insight that had come to me.

'Say then that we met so and talked, and that you showed me something for which I have no name. Grant all that and then ask whether between us money is a thing worthy of notice. I am not rich, but a sum like that can make no difference at all to me, while to Jake it will make a great deal. Aren't we agreed on the unimportance of physical things? Let's be thorough and despise money.'

'You are right,' she said at last. 'I have never seen anyone quite like you. I think I shall remember you always. And if there is ever anything that money or service can do to help you or your cause, remember the Great Harry, Welland, Norfolk. We're in touch with France and other places, and it's the best hiding-place in the world. And it belongs to me. You will remember.'

How could I ever forget, I wondered, as I stooped over her hand. I meant to see her again, to find the Great Harry, to – oh, but what didn't I intend to do?

And the years passed and yesterday I heard a boy humming a tune and I didn't for hours remember the tune or where I had heard it. It is a very bitter thing to grow old and to forget such things as this. Very bitter indeed, I assure you.

RENÉ DE VIPONT ST. HELIER TELLS HIS STORY 'THERE IS A TAVERN' A.D. 1800

CHAPTER FIVE

THE FRENCHMAN

WE give our mistresses jewels and carriages and money at times and compliments at all times, and we give our wives our names and our homes and our children . . . we are never really loved. It is not until a man has nothing to give to a woman, not even his presence, that he can say that he has been truly loved. We in France before the Revolution held love very lightly, as we held all things except maybe position and power; it was born with help of soft lights, sweet music, and idleness; it lived awhile, fed on intrigue and scandal; it died, and we covered the corpse with laughter and a new *affaire*. Perhaps that was as well – there was pain in the thought of lips even lightly kissed falling stiff and pale on to the sawdust in the Place de la Révolution; if we had loved deeply, with that passion that loses sight of humour and proportion, then indeed how deep would have been our agony! Two instead of one would have died at each falling of the guillotine. And such a love brushed past me so closely that a little of that agony has remained with me until this day.

It was in connection with a counter-revolutionary plot that I first set foot in England. I carried with me certain secret papers and was to bring back signatures, documents, promises, and gold. It was, needless to add, a journey demanding the utmost secrecy. I was landed upon a desolate part of the Norfolk coast, surely the bleakest spot upon this earth; from there I was to make my way to Bedford, a small town easterly enough to be within easy reach of the coast, yet central enough to enable me to get in touch with the men I wanted. From there it was possible that I might have to go to London. To await my coming a ship, named *La Belle Louise,* was to lie off the coast at a certain point on the 14th of December; if I did not meet her on that night, she was to leave, in case her prolonged stay should promote inquiry, and to return on the night of the 20th. I regret to burden the story by these details, but they are needed to the perfect understanding of the tale.

It was not necessary for me to proceed to London, so on the night of the 14th I set out with the precious documents and money concealed about me. A rowboat that belonged to an old and tried associate was engaged to take me to the ship; and as I had now no fears and had slept but very little for six or seven nights before, as soon as I was seated in the boat I fell into a light doze. I cannot therefore tell exactly what happened, but I was awakened from my doze to find myself violently turned out of the boat into the icy water; and although we shouted to one another, the wind and the rain and the darkness made barriers between us, so what happened to the boatman is another thing that I shall never know. I hope he escaped, for he was a very honest man. I am a fair, though not good swimmer, and the water was extremely cold, but the thought of my mission and the precious papers upon me enabled me to put up a desperate struggle. But all my real and almost all my false strength was exhausted and I could imagine my bloated corpse washing up somewhere on that lonely coast, when I heard the sound of dipping oars and, gathering together every atom of force left in me, I raised a despairing shout. I heard the oars stop as the men who wielded them listened, and, much enheartened, I called again. In a very few minutes a strong hand seized first my hair, then the collar of my coat, and I was dragged bodily into a large boat rowed by two men. To them I explained my accident, and offered them gold if they would turn and row me out to the waiting ship. This they would not do, although in an eagerness that almost proved my later undoing I sent up my price, offering them what must have seemed extravagant sums. But they in turn said that their errand was urgent, that the wind would shortly be blowing a gale, that I had had one ducking and might be content for the night. So at last, shivering in my wet clothes and miserably uncertain in my mind, I offered them even larger sums if they would take me ashore, find me some safe lodging, and row me out to *La Belle Louise* on the night of the 20th. It seemed then that I should be not so much worse off than I should have been if I had had to continue my journey to London. One of the men said:

'Don't you worry, monsieur, we're used to keeping secrets and you won't be the first lodger to stay at the Great Harry without wanting to look outside.' On this speech the other man, whom I judged to be the elder, shot out his foot and landed the other a kick, after which there was no more conversation; I sat and tried to control the chattering of my teeth, and presently the man who had kicked his companion drew in his oars, divested himself of his coat, and wrapped it warmly around me. It smelt not unpleasantly of sea-water and onions and tobacco.

At last the boat grated upon a sandy beach, the two men leaped out, and I followed as nimbly as I was able, being now almost rigid with cold and dampness. The elder man said something to the younger in a patois that I did not understand, although my general English is fluent and good, and then turned and led the way over a great deal of sand and some long rough grass towards a house with lighted windows and a sign creaking over the door; this I judged to be the Great Harry, where guests were lodged and no questions asked. My guide threw open a door and said: 'Mind the step.'

I put out a cautious foot and landed in a passage some eighteen inches below the level of the threshold. Light outlined the cracks of a door on my left, and from behind it came the sound of laughter and voices and of heavily shod feet moving on a sanded floor; the passage smelt, rather like the coat, of onions and tobacco with the addition of beer. We went down the whole length of this passage and through a low door that opened upon a great stone-floored kitchen; an enormous fire burned at the far end of it, and my first impulse was to run towards it, kneel by it, and stretch out my numb hands. But there were several people in the kitchen, women amongst them, and possibly my future hostess, so I stopped on the threshold, with a little bow. The man with me thrust me forward, slammed the door and strode towards the fireplace. He scowled round him with evident disfavour.

'Let's see the fire,' he said in a growl, and spurned the great logs with his wet boots. One of the women stood up sulkily, and I sat down with much gratitude close to the leaping flames.

'Who is it, Andy?' asked a thin but not unpleasant voice. I looked towards the speaker and saw a very old woman seated in the high-backed armchair in the opposite corner of the hearth.

'A Frenchman, Mother. We picked him out of the water. Would one of you just stir yourselves and get us something to drink? What will you have, monsieur, gin or brandy?'

'Brandy,' I said, yearning towards the warmth that the word promised. One of the women, a down-at-heel trollop, shuffled over to a cupboard in the corner and returned with a bottle and two glasses. Andy half filled the glasses, added boiling water from the kettle that stood steaming on the hob, and handed one to me with a certain graciousness of gesture that rather surprised me. Not so much, however, as the brandy did; it was the very best, and ran round my veins and gladdened my heart with warmth and comfort. The old woman now began to rail at the women around her.

'He must go to bed at once in hot blankets. Is there not one of all you fat helpless creatures who could think of that? What a thing it is to be old and helpless and surrounded with wenches that haven't a thought outside their bellies! Where is Charlotte? Andy, where is your daughter?'

'In the bar, Mother.'

'Then send her to me at once. Why is she to be always there? Can't Susan, the fat sow, be trusted to draw pints of slush for muddy yokels?'

'All right, all right,' said Andy. 'Kitty, go to the bar and send Charlotte here.'

As soon as Kitty's grudging exit had been made, the old woman went on: 'French, did you say? Is he handsome?'

'Fair to middling,' Andy answered with a glance at me, and added in a softer tone: 'She's blind.'

'I regret,' I said, and looked more closely at the old woman; I should not have guessed very readily why she referred to herself as 'helpless', for there was nothing unusual about her eyes, not even that stare which often betrays sightlessness when there is nothing else to do so. Her eyes were beautifully shaped and curiously coloured, a clear bluish green, a colour I have seen in cats' eyes in broad daylight. They showed up more startlingly for the fact that her face was a mere brown network of wrinkles, with jutting cheek-bones, nose, and chin. A face that had once perhaps been beautiful . . . I gave a little sigh at this evidence of the destructiveness, the inevitability of age.

Then suddenly the door was opened, more quietly than anyone had opened it yet, and the girl whom they called Charlotte came in. I had seen many of the fairest women in France and in Spain, and in Poland, where they are very fair indeed; I had seen Marie Antionette and that Josephine whom Napoleon loved and many others less easily named because of the sorrow that their names recall; but I had never seen then, nor, I think, have I seen since, a woman more lovely than this daughter of a squalid inn. Ah, Charlotte, would that I were a poet! Then my words could call you so vividly to mind that you might enjoy a little immortality, even after all these years. It was not only the clear, smooth, golden skin, beneath which the colour lay, a pale vermilion; it was not the black hair so glossy smooth, nor the proud thin arch of the eyebrows over the copper brown of her eyes; nor was it the slender strength of her neck and form. No, a woman may have all this and more, and yet miss the beauty that shone in this one.

'Come along, deary,' said the old woman coaxingly. 'I want you to make a warm bed for our guest.'

There was a strange beseeching quality in the old voice. I thought that the grandmother loved Charlotte a great deal and was not always sure of her obedience; yet the words 'our guest' had a gracious sound, might have been those of a great lady with unbounded means of hospitality at her disposal. Charlotte turned at once to me, and I was unable to change my wondering stare into a casual glance quickly enough; the colour deepened in her cheeks. Without a word she went out of the room and returned with a bundle of blankets upon her arm. She knelt and held them to the fire, Andy replenished our glasses, a baby in a wooden cradle behind the old woman's chair began to wail, and one of the women who had been talking softly together rose and began to suckle it without any sign of modesty. I was almost asleep where I sat and Andy must have seen my state, for he said, less gruffly than he had spoken to the others: 'That will do, girl, take them upstairs and show him the way.'

'Let me carry them,' I said, but she shook her head and walked before me to the door. Then I suddenly understood her colouring, her shape, her grace, for her walk bore witness to a streak of West Indian blood. I had noticed it in Paris a hundred times – a girl with no face, no figure, no conversation, would radiate this inexplicable charm; you would inquire and find every time that her family had had business in the West Indies, and that somewhere amongst her ancestresses was a smooth brown woman to whom she owed it all. Odd, because some of the full-blooded native women whom I have seen have lacked it entirely. It is a question of a mere suspicion, like the pinch of salt that makes all the difference to coffee.

I turned to Andy from this contemplation of his daughter's back.

'Good night,' I said. 'I owe my life to your timely aid, I am not unconscious of that.'

'All right. Good night,' he said, and waved his hand as if in dismissal. When I said good night to the old woman, I saluted her skinny brown claw. She gave an almost coquettish laugh and cried: 'I am sure he is handsome; I can feel if I cannot see.'

Charlotte, as I turned, was watching from the doorway with an expression of supreme scorn upon her face.

The stairs were of wood and very twisted. At the top was a passage and at the end of it a room, drearier even than the kitchen downstairs; that at least was warm, but this apartment, with its ill-fitting window and open fireplace, was horribly cold and, in the light of Charlotte's one candle, a little sinister too. She spread the blankets upon the bed with rapid gestures that never once ceased to be beautiful; but her hands, I noticed almost with sorrow, were red and roughened with the work she did. When at last she raised one of them to stroke back a lock of hair that had fallen as she leaned over the bed, the proximity of such a hand to such a face had about it something almost grotesque. She said good night in a brief unfriendly way and was gone.

Such was my introduction to the family at the Great Harry; I thought of the name again as I fell asleep. I wondered if perhaps it were named after Henry Tudor, a king of England during the time of our King Francis.

In the morning I awoke to the scent of coffee, a beverage I had not hoped to taste until I reached Boulogne again. Charlotte stood by my bed, her expression still sullen.

'I've brought your coffee, and your clothes will be dry presently.'

I was rather piqued by her manner, so chill and unsmiling. I despise coxcombry, yet at the same time I am little used to being looked on so coldly. I was moreover conscious of having been taken at a disadvantage, having just awakened. But I thanked her for the coffee and inquired who had been so kind as to remove my sodden clothes while I slept. She answered that she had done so, and turning at the door, said:

'How are you? – Grandmother is asking.' In other words, she had no interest in my well-being or otherwise; but then why emphasize it so?

'I am perfectly well. Thank Madame your grandmother for her kind inquiries,' I said, and buried my face in my coffee-cup, a gesture of dismissal that I should have liked to make earlier, but could not until her back was turned, lying as I did naked in the bed.

After that I slept for another half-hour and was awakened this time by discordant voices in the passage outside. I heard the grandmother say in her authoritative voice: 'Go at once; do as I tell you'; and Charlotte in an equally shrill voice said: 'I will not; take them yourself, or let somebody else. Why should I be his servant?' Next came the sound of a sharp blow, as of a cheek being smartly slapped; then there was silence again. Presently a heavy slipshod footstep came towards my door and stopped outside. Susan entered carrying my clothes, which had been sponged, dried, and very well pressed, and a razor and a jug of hot water. This was indeed far better treatment than I had dared to hope for, and I gave Susan my best thanks.

As soon as I was dressed I went down, to find the blind woman sitting as before by the fire, but she was alone in the kitchen. When I had greeted her I inquired the name of the family, for it struck me that, could I favourably impress Andy, he might be a valuable assistant to us in future, for his inn was just the place for quiet comings and goings; and I did not feel that the best way to win his favour was by addressing him as 'Andy'. I explained this to the old woman, who said: 'Oh, call him anything, he'd never notice, he's a good boy, Andy, the best of all my sons, but he lost his head as well as his heart and has never been the same since. Oh, yes, the name is Winfarthing. . . . All the men get married and none of the women do, so we're all Winfarthings.' She accompanied this remark with a little chuckle.

I looked through the window, which looked inland; my bedroom window had looked towards the sea, so I had now a comprehensive idea of the situation of the inn. Inland were miles of sand, very barely covered by sparse grass and sea-thistle. Far away I could see the dark line of the leafless woods. The house itself was whitewashed and streaked with damp and had a deep thatch greened over with moss. It was very old and gloomy, but an excellent hiding-place.

I was soon very bored with looking out of the window, and I wished to see Charlotte, partly as one wishes always to gaze again on a thing that one has had time but briefly to admire, partly because I wanted to make her talk. She could, if she would, have told me many interesting things, why she herself was so different, so like the women of San Domingo; why the blind grandmother had such authority; these and many other questions, of no importance but much interest, teased my ever lively sense of curiosity.

The old woman presently said sharply: 'Don't wander about like that, you annoy me. If you are wanting Charlotte, she's through that door there.' She waved her brown claw, and I followed its direction and opened the door. Within was a scullery, and here in a greasy, smoky cell was Charlotte, peeling potatoes, her hands all crimson and swollen from long immersion in water and across her cheek four red marks, the remains of the blow that I had heard. And that was because of me. I know that people of other nations mock at the susceptibility of the French, and I am aware that possibly an Englishman or a German or a Dane would have viewed those marks with far less emotion, and yet later on have behaved very differently; however we are as we are, and I stood aghast at the sight of such beauty, engaged in such menial work and wearing upon her face the print of angry fingers. The peeled potatoes she threw into a great black saucepan and a pigs' pail stood near by for the peelings. I was not quite sure how to begin, and while I stood just looking at her, she whirled round on me in a fury.

'Must you follow me even here to gloat at me?' she cried. I was nonplussed.

'Mademoiselle,' I said, 'nothing could be farther from my wishes than to follow you, or to gloat over you. Why should I? I came partly to tell you that I overheard this morning, and to assure you that I should never regard anything that you might do for me as other than a high honour that you confer upon me. The warm bed last night saved my life, the coffee this morning gave me back my balance, and the clothes so admirably restored enable me to present myself decently before you this morning. All the services you have done me have made me very deeply your debtor; I owe you moreover gratitude for your beauty, for that is indeed a gift which its possessors bestow continually upon their fellows.'

Perhaps it was the studied gentleness of my speech, or regret at her anger, or merely the effect of nerves overwrought – I know not, but her eyes softened and filled with tears, and her lovely lips quivered. She dropped the potato and the knife which she was handling, and, turning as far from me as the space would permit, she fumbled with her apron. I realized that she had no handkerchief and, chiefly in fear for her lest, reduced to using her apron, she might experience some of her queer shame, I offered her mine, roughly dried as it was and salty, having been overlooked in the charitable ministrations of the night before. Once having begun to cry, she went on and on; but at last I laid my hand upon her shoulder, turned her towards me, and brushing back the hair from her flushed face, stroked her cheek with my fingers. And in that moment I realized that my admiration for her, which had led me to think of her hands as a blemish, had given way to a profound pity, which made those rough red hands as appealing to me as would be the cut knee of a little child.

'Tell me, little one,' I said, 'is anything really wrong, or are you overwrought? Is there no one here who can do anything but you? . . .' But before I could even finish my inquiry, she had seen a shadow pass by the tiny window.

'Quick, there's Simon, get into the kitchen before he can get through the door.'

Here was another mystery; but I was even then too old a hand to wait and ask questions when a lady says 'Go,' so I was already in the kitchen with the old blind woman when Simon opened the kitchen door. I had not seen him before; he had red hair, and the old woman's beaky nose and prominent cheek-bones – Scots blood, I thought. He sat down, removed his boots, and stuck out his feet to the fire, without saying a word to the grandmother, if such she was to him, not to me. When his not very fragrant stockings were steaming he put on his boots again and made off towards the bar. The old woman looked at me with an expression of cunning and a kind of sympathy upon her face, which I found most embarrassing; it was as if, seeing nothing, she saw all things and had known how the touch of her granddaughter's hair under my hand had quickened my breathing, and that I had been unceremoniously banished from the scullery because the red-headed lout had passed the window.

I began to wish that my exile were over. I opened a conversation with the old woman for the want of something better to do, and at once the hateful expression was banished from her face and was replaced by one of deep intelligent attention. At her request I described my clothes, my features, the streets of Paris, Madrid, and Warsaw. She had a very sharp inquiring mind. So the time rolled along to dinner, when Susan, and Kitty, and the woman with the baby, and Andy and George, who had rescued me, and Simon, and Charlotte, with a half-wit boy whose name I never learned, all sat down to a plentiful meal of boiled rabbit and salt pork, well cooked but roughly served. There were also potatoes, which I refused. They fingered their food, gnawing the rabbit bones, and having reduced them to a certain bareness, handed them under the table to the lurcher dogs that cringed there. Yet they served me as their guest first and refrained from speech when their mouths were full, a fact which caused me infinite relief.

The thought of the long afternoon appalled me, but like an old campaigner I decided to take advantage of a slack time to sleep; so I wrapped myself in my blankets and slept until long after dark. I then descended and sat by the fire, eating bread and cheese for supper and drinking ale. Charlotte was not about and I found it difficult to sustain conversation with the blind woman, with the blank face of Susan, Kitty, and the half-wit staring at me. At eleven o'clock I went thankfully to bed, but I had slept too long in the afternoon and now lay wakeful long after the last stumbling customer had gone home.

And now comes a part of my story that may sound incredible to you, as indeed it seemed to me when it happened, making me think for a moment that their ale was more potent than I had believed.

My door opened very softly and someone sheltering a candle in her hand came in. The movement in my blood assured me that it was Charlotte. She was wearing a long white gown and had a dark cloak thrown over her shoulders. The candle sent waves of light and shade across her face, as the flame waved in the draught that blew from the window.

I raised myself on my elbow and said:

'My dear child, what do you think you're doing here?'

Without answering she blew out the candle and threw herself on the bed beside me. I began to make some half-hearted protest and then she spoke. 'I knew it,' she said, with a hissing intake of her breath; 'if you hadn't seen me making beds and washing dishes, you would have thought I was pretty, you would have wanted me to come.'

'That's nonsense,' I said sharply. 'I told you this morning that I admire you very much.'

'But you don't like me?'

'It's not that either.' I began to feel that I was handling this situation very badly. I tried to imagine Claude or Charles in this position ... but I knew what they would do and I knew in my heart then that I was going to do the same. Hesitation was fatal; her arms, bared of the cloak, and cool, went round my neck. She whispered that she loved me the moment that she saw me; that was why she had so hated me to see her at her lowly tasks. And I had been so long absent from my home, busy about things in which women played no part, and her warmth and slenderness were under my hands, her hair on my eyes, and her lips on my mouth. The most frigid Puritan would have succumbed – as I did. Once a horrible pang shook me, a return of that pity which is so alien to physical pleasure ... but someone must be first! And the old woman had said that the women never married. It was not, I told myself, as if I were seducing a cloistered, sheltered demoiselle and ruining her for all time. So I banished at once my scruples and my pity.

When I awoke she had gone, but the candle stood on the floor. Doubts and regrets nagged me again. I repeated my comfortable reasoning, adding that it was an unexpected visitation and an uninvited one. I was amazed that twenty-four hours of my proximity should have engendered the frenzy of adoration of which I had just had such ample proof.

I was not really comforted.

When during the day I was once more alone in the kitchen with the old blind woman, she said, in the middle of a talk on quite another subject: 'André's father was a very gallant soldier; I am glad that André's daughter is one to know something better than a drunken yokel's pawings.'

'She told you?' I asked sickly.

'Of course not; there are some things that one does not have to be told.'

I thought of all the dowagers who glare from the walls, mindful that one does not dance too often with their charges or lead them out to balcony or garden. And suddenly I saw that their attitude is right; a virgin, I thought, is a thing to watch and guard, not to give away to the first stranger. And yet the old woman's manner and calmness saved this attitude, which would have been obscene in anyone else, from seeming so in her.

We had three nights of perfect and delightful intimacy. I found her mind no less stimulating than her body, her ideas were so rare and strange. She faced the idea of spending the rest of her life in that hovel with the utmost calm. I protested against it, and she said:

'I love the Great Harry, I am free here. There is the sea and in the summer the woods, full of cuckoos. I could leave here to be two things in the world. I could be an honest servant or a dishonest woman. I can be that here. After all, one loves but once. Beyond that once what does it matter whether one does it for diamonds in a great city or for a whim in one's home?'

I admitted the evident if rather sorry truth of that. She told me that Simon had been waiting for her for years, but that she herself had been waiting too. I inquired for what.

'For you, René, oh, the dear little name. I knew you must come – everybody has something, once.'

There was truth in that too. Even in that most tragic of stories, before Cavalry there was the shouting and the palm-strewn streets of Jerusalem. Ah, Charlotte, there was great wisdom and great delight in you. And from pity, which from me to you was an insult, I passed to new admiration. You were poor and a woman and infatuate, but you were my superior, you faced your life as it was, you took what you wanted, in the ultimate issue you did what you chose. And how few of us can honestly say that?

On the fourth night she came to me troubled, so vaguely that I think that many men would not have noticed the slight wavering of her attention . . . but I am a connoisseur in these matters. Next day a stranger called to see Andy, and they paced up and down before the house, talking very earnestly. Then he came in and said that he would not be able to fulfil his bargain personally, as the stranger had brought news of a job which demanded the attention of himself and George; but Simon, he said, would see that I reached *La Belle Louise* in safety. Remembering the bundles in the boat that rescued me, the way that they handled old French brandy as if it were water, and the way in which they said the few French words I heard them use, I came to the conclusion that they were smugglers and that a job, for George and Andy, meant a cargo, which naturally couldn't wait.

That night Charlotte questioned me. Was it quite imperative, she queried, that I should leave on the Friday night? This inquiry I put down to the natural reluctance of a loving woman to face her lover's going; I hoped that she was not going to prove difficult. I began to reckon up the debt that I owed the Fates for those happy nights. I replied firmly that it was quite imperative. Contrary to my fears, she said no more about it, but she was for some time very distrait.

'Something troubles you, *ma petite*?' I said.

'It is only my imagination. I think I must go now.'

I told her that the night was yet young, and the time remaining to us all too brief. The thought that in a few hours I should see her no more lent eloquence to my tongue; but with a set and almost stony face she turned away, relighted her candle, and left me. Caprice, I thought, and marvelled that it was a quality inseparable from charm. From the thought of our parting I passed to the contemplation of my journey tomorrow, the final completion of my mission, the joyful welcome that awaited me. I was suddenly anxious to be gone, to move once more in a world where men spoke and thought as I did. I realized that for five days I had had no interest outside the person of a country girl, who had probably never heard the name of Bourbon.

By this time sleep had deserted me and I found that my nerves were so strained that the creaking of the floor as I turned in my bed seemed a noise almost unbearable. The sudden closing of a door startled me violently, there was a stealthy step outside – a step to which in my ordinary state I should have been quite oblivious. Tonight its stealthiness gave it potency. I ran to my door and with equal stealth opened it just an inch. Charlotte was creeping down the half-flight of stairs that led to Simon's room. She held the candle low to light her steps and with the fingers of her other hand she lightly brushed her eyelashes. There, to all appearances alone on the deserted stairs in the middle of the sleeping house, she brushed her eyes with a gesture that had in it the whole secret of beauty. I had an impulse to drag her inside my door, I wanted to know why she had gone from me, whom she protested to love, to the red-headed cousin; I wanted to know why she came away crying. Most of all I wanted to bury my hands in her hair, shake her, hurt her, kiss her. But I had no right to question any of her actions or to dispute the distribution of her favours. I stepped back, the light of the candle fell in a line upon my floor, and then passed on. I went and threw myself on my bed, a little relieved that I had seen this proof of her looseness; it eased a sorrow that had eaten unwelcomed into my reason, whenever I thought of her.

Just before dark on the next day Andy and George departed; I said farewell to them and gave Andy the sum upon which we had agreed. He thanked me, bade Charlotte see that we had a hot meal before we set out, wished me *bon voyage*, and slouched away. I wanted to give Charlotte a ring which I always wore upon my fourth finger, a sentimental gesture that satisfied my sense of fitness, so I went to the stair-foot and beckoned to her. She followed me with a reluctant obedience, and when we stood together behind the closed door of my room she neither spoke to nor looked at me, but stood, holding her elbows with her hands, pressing her arms close to her body as if she were very cold.

'I wanted to say good-bye to you away from the others; I wanted also to give you this,' and upon my palm I held out to her the ring, with the fox's head carved upon its still green surface. I had valued the ring and loved it; for a little I had loved the girl and it was fitting that I should leave them both here upon this desolate coast, washed by the two grey tides of sand and water. She took the ring and held it towards the light, looking at it with attentive admiration.

'It is lovely, and valuable,' she said at length, 'but I don't want it.'

'Oh, come!' I said, combating what I imagined to be natural diffidence. 'I wish particularly that you should have it as a keepsake. As for its loveliness, it is fitting that you should have it; as for its value, you may easily have more precious ones some day, but wear it a little even then in memory of me.'

But she laid the ring upon the chest beside her and walked to the window and stood there, looking out into the dark, as if she were listening to some voice that I could not hear. And still staring at the darkened panes, she spoke.

'You must say good-bye to me here, because Simon does not know that you are anything to me, but I shall see you again, because I am coming to the ship with you. Evil is awaiting you, though what it is I do not know; a storm perhaps, then we could drown together. Or not a storm, something from which a friendly hand might save you. It's a feeling, it is in this family to know things before they happen, it is weak in me, I cannot know clearly; if Grandmother had been in my place she would have known it all. Still, I know. Last night I went to Simon; I thought he might tell me something, give me some clue, but he said nothing; only he says that I may come with you, partly because he is lazy and would like my help with the boat, partly because he thinks that after last night I am so crazy in love with him that I cannot bear him out of my sight.' She laughed, and at the same moment the voice of Susan came bellowing up the stairs to say that the coffee was made. Charlotte turned to me then and flung her arms round me with a convulsive pressure.

'Good-bye, my dear, my dear, my dear,' she whispered, and, turning, she picked up the ring. 'I shall not need anything like this to remember you by. Give it to someone with white hands.' And in a moment she was through the door and running lightly along the passage and downstairs. I followed, feeling foolish and troubled.

The coffee, well laced with brandy, awaited us with a meal of hot fish, in deference to my having refused meat at midday, it being Friday. We ate standing and I bethought me of the Passover of the Jews.

Charlotte unhooked a great rough sea-cloak from behind the scullery door and turned up the collar, so that only the top of her shining head showed above it. I put on my coat, Simon lighted the lantern, and we were ready. For the last time I bent over the old woman's brown hand. I thanked her once more for her hospitality to me.

She said in her thin voice: 'Better luck this time, monsieur; you are in good hands.'

Once out in the open, I felt the full force of the wind, but at least it was no longer crying like a thing possessed, as it had done at every door and window of the inn. I offered to row, but Simon said: 'Better not; Charlotte's used to it.'

They rowed for a long time in silence, then Charlotte began to sing softly, in time with her strokes. I asked her what it was, for I could catch only shreds of it. She laughed again. 'You can learn it,' she said, 'it's very small:

'Always they show him small
Naked and fair and blind,
That we, on meeting him,
Should still be kind.

Yet in that same small hand
Arrows full sharp he had,
That we, on leaving him.
Should still be sad.'

'That isn't what I call a good song,' grumbled Simon; 'it doesn't mean anything.'

Soon he stopped and said: 'What was the signal?'

I told him, and he said: 'Change places with me, Charlotte,' and when she had done so with the careful nimbleness of one to whom movement in an unsteady boat was no new thing, he stooped and fumbled in the tarpaulin at the bottom of the boat as if for the lantern; but when he straightened himself he held instead a short thick bludgeon.

It all happened so suddenly that it was like the vivid moment that one experiences in a dream at the moment before waking. He aimed a deadly blow at me. I tried to withdraw my hands, which were buried in my pockets, and then, with his blow undelivered, he fell over the side of the boat, brought down by a blow which Charlotte aimed at his knee with the butt of her oar. It was all over before I could get my hands clear of my pockets; in an almost unbroken movement he fell into the water, turned over and clutched the side of the boat. It rocked, I threw my weight instinctively towards the other side, while Charlotte with a deliberate movement stabbed at the white face with the oar.

It was rather a horrible thing to see. His hands gave way, an awful cry came up from the water, she stabbed again, there was a last thrashing in the sea, and then stillness. In that silence she sat down again.

'So that was it,' she said slowly.

'He would have killed me,' I said.

'Yes, it was well planned, wasn't it? Your body overboard, your money in their pockets. Not a trace. Oh, he's a clever man, my father, and you see Simon has paid for his cleverness. Wasn't it well that I came?'

'Assuredly I owe you my life,' I said, and I thought of the dead man out there, floating with his battered face . . . that might have been me.

Charlotte with the lantern was making the signal; and I sat in the stupor of no feeling that follows a brief, sharp period of great feeling. I did not even bother to look out for the answering light, but I heard Charlotte give a little satisfied sigh as she settled down again to her rowing. I wanted to speak to her, but my tongue would utter none of the endearments that I had been accustomed to use to her; for she had suddenly assumed in my sight a grand and rather terrible aspect. I managed at last to say what was uppermost in my mind:

'You will never be able to go back.'

'Why not? There was a struggle about something that I did not understand, and you both went overboard. Was I to blame?'

I knew that I should for many reasons ask her to come with me, but I thought of the future, of the plot whose young being lay awaiting birth in the papers in my breast; I realized that in the wild upheaval that we had planned there was no place for her or for any woman other than those whose business is the temporary pleasure of men whose hearts are elsewhere. And as if she could indeed read my mind she said lightly:

'Why do you feel responsible for me now? Because of a movement of my arm that cost me nothing? Surely that was a lesser thing.'

I understood what she meant and once again that little worm of shame wriggled within my heart. What was I, after all, to have laid such fantastic sins upon her?

The dark hull of *La Belle Louise* was now directly ahead and then alongside of us, with the ladder swinging and a cluster of heads about its side.

'Then,' I began, 'it is really good-bye at last. I have no words . . . I shall remember you always.'

I recalled all the partings of my lifetime. Never was one so strange or so hopeless – no '*Au revoir*', nothing.

'Good-bye,' she said, 'be careful of your life in the years that are coming and enjoy it . . . you owe me that.'

On the silky surface of the water her boat made an unshining patch; I heard, or imagined that I heard for a moment, the sound of her oars. Then both sight and sound were swallowed in the darkness – that was the end. But I have not forgotten – I am old now and broken, with nothing to offer to anyone . . . but once, you see, I was loved, as few men are.

AGNES TRUDGETT TELLS THE STORY OF A WILD FLOWER TRANSPLANTED A.D. 1830

CHAPTER SIX

WILD FLOWER TRANSPLANTED

WE all knew that Master John and the mistress had had a terrible row; they'd both got loud voices, so we always knew when they disagreed. They'd both got very fierce stubborn tempers, too, so that I often thought how clever it was of the old master to leave her most of the money, and him the Manor; for most of their rows ended fairly quickly, because he was always in need of money and she was very fond of the Manor, so it paid them both to settle their differences. In fact, after a row they used to be very good friends, and she'd give him money to spend on his horses, and he'd give way about the rock garden, or the pond that she'd been wanting to put in the garden.

But this row went on and on. The butler, who heard more than he should, as I often had cause to tell him, said it was about a young lady named Renée, which sounded French to me; perhaps that was why we'd none of us heard her name before. When the quarrel had lasted about four days, we knew that it must be serious; and so it was, for Mrs. Audley suddenly ordered all her things to be packed and went all round the house collecting the bits of china and furniture that were hers; and we understood that she was leaving for good. I for one was very sorry to hear it, for she'd been the only person who had any control over Master John since his father died, and Heaven knew that he needed controlling.

On the afternoon of the day that his mother went

away, he came up to the little room that had been his old nursery, and which was now mine, where I did all the mending and suchlike jobs, and said:

'Agnes, I want to talk to you.'

'Talk away, then, Master John, I can listen as I sew,' I said.

'I'm going to be married.' Well, I had rather expected that, but I didn't feel any cause to say so.

'Who to, sir?'

'Her name is Renée Winfarthing; she comes from your way, you may know her.'

'You don't mean to tell me that you're going to marry a girl from the Great Harry. Oh no, Master John, you'll have to tell me another tale from that.'

'Well, that's what I *am* telling you. And if you want to look like that about it, you'd better pack all your things and get off before I quarrel with you.'

I'd known him ever since he was born; before that, almost, you might say; and I knew from when he was a little thing it was no good crossing him when he'd got that pucker on his forehead and his lip sticking out so. So I said:

'Very well, Master John. Was that all you wanted to say to me?'

'No, not half. Mother has gone, as you know. When she can promise to be pleasant to my wife, she can come back if she wants to; until then I must arrange for someone to take charge of things; it will all be a little strange to her at first. You can have the job if you like; only remember – no more long faces or raised eyebrows, because I won't have them. How do you feel about that? Can you manage?'

I stopped my work, and I said:

'I've known you, Master John, so long that you must forgive me if what I'm going to say now is out of place. May I just speak out for once, and then, if you won't heed what I say, I'll be quiet about it and do my best to run the house as it has been run and keep you and your lady comfortable? I know that you young men get away from the country into London and mix with a lot of people with new ideas, and then you think that you've seen life and know a lot better on every question that an old woman like me, or even than a lady like your mother, who's always led a quiet respectable life. And I dare say that to you now the idea of marrying for love, and hang the consequences, seems a grand thing, in keeping with all these new poetical fancies of yours. That's where you're wrong and where you make fair game of yourself for women like those at the Great Harry. Why, sir, not one of them's been properly married in the memory of man; they're loose from the moment they cease to be children – and that's early enough with that mixed gypsy breed. This one you say you're going to marry, she's Charlotte's daughter, unless my memory fails me, but who was her father? Do you know? Does anybody? I shouldn't think Charlotte knew herself. Even if this girl is all right herself, what kind of blood do you think she has in her and what kind of a bringing-up has she had? A real bad mother, two drunken aunts or whatever they are, and men in and out of the place all hours. Now, don't be angry with me, sir, but take my advice. Have your fling with her, that's what they're used to, they'd understand; or if you've got into a bit of a mess with her, buy yourself out, it'd be the cheapest way and the best. Not marrying one of that kind. Don't you run the risk of leaving the Manor and all that'll be yours presently to a child with Winfarthing blood. It's too bad; why, they don't stop at murder, and they smuggle, and I have even heard tell that once one of them married a black woman, leastways brown. That's a very old story, but they're often true stories in these out-of-the-way places.'

I stopped then, for I could see the cloud deepen on his face, and I thought the next thing would be an order for me to up stick and go. But the cloud suddenly cleared and he laughed.

'You're a fine old hypocrite, aren't you, Agnes? Running down their ways and then bidding me take any of the alternatives to the honourable marriage that I intend. Listen, have you ever seen a flower that's taken root in a muckheap? – it's often much finer than its neighbour growing on the path. I think that that illustrates this case. Now we are going to transplant it, in a manner of speaking, and you must help. There's not to be a word of this to anyone else, nor a sign in your manner that you know anything. I shall have to get rid of one or two of the women in the house, and a man or so outside; and some of the horses will have to go too. But we shall manage. I think, now you've to be in the kitchen more, you'd better have a room on the first floor to save your legs a bit. That's all.'

There was always that about Master John; he had a quick temper and a masterful manner, but he was considerate, as lots of pleasanter people aren't. I tried to remember having seen this Winfarthing girl, but I hadn't been home to Welland since my father died, and even then the people from the Great Harry hardly ever came into the village; but I seemed to recollect seeing that fat Susan going through the churchyard with a dark gypsy-looking girl with her. I thought that I shouldn't enjoy calling her 'Madam'. We'd always been respectable in my family. Still, no one else would want to employ an old woman whose best days had been spent in someone else's service, and if she was good enough for Master John to marry . . .

And married they were. He went off in the carriage that he'd had all newly painted, and where the money was coming from I wondered. Then from Brighton I received a long letter all about what time they'd be home and what I was to get ready. If the evening was cold for June, there was to be a fire in the dining-room and another in the drawing-room; there was to be one in the bedroom in any case. The gardener was to bring in the very best of the roses and there were to be some of those in the bedroom too. But the chests in the hall were to have gillyflowers in bowls, and the hound, Spartan, who could not be relied upon to join in the welcome was to be banished to the stables. There seemed to be no detail too small to be thought of. I was fairly crazed. And if it had been for Miss Isabel or even Lady Rosemary, though I didn't like her so well, I wouldn't have minded, but all this fuss over a girl who had served drink in an inn, it seemed foolish to me. However, I carried out the orders as I was paid to do, and at last the afternoon came for the return of the master and the entrance of the mistress.

There was a clatter of hoofs and the jingle of harness, and there was the master lifting her down from the carriage and across the threshold into the great hall. I stepped up and made my curtsy, sore against my will, as you may imagine; but she smiled at me and said: 'Oh yes, John says you come from Welland too. That's nice.' A brassy thing to say, I thought; if we were willing to forget Welland, surely she might have been. She was the girl I'd seen in the churchyard, though of course altered by being dressed in fashionable clothes and having her hair done properly. She had an odd face, old for a girl of nineteen or twenty, which at the outside she could only have been; it was dark and sulky, but she had long eyelashes, a very red mouth, and a cluster of shining curls on each temple; there was nothing that the master couldn't have matched twenty times amongst the ladies in the county. She'd no figure at all, though the London frock did its best to hide that; very cunningly tucked it was and tied with cherry-coloured ribbons that matched her mouth.

'We're famished,' said the master, and hurried her away upstairs, while I went off into the kitchen, where of course everybody was all excitement.

The newness wore off, and I must say that by the end of the week no one had anything but praise for her. Barber would come grinning out of the dining-room and repeat the funny things that she said to make the master laugh, and Flossie could talk of nothing but her hair, how long and soft it was and how naturally it waved. And I must say that the master improved too, losing all his old sulky looks, and head over ears in love with her, plain for all men to see.

It was a fortnight before they had any difference of opinion, and I wondered whether that was the first time she'd come up against his stubborn temper. He'd bought, almost the minute he was back, a lovely little white mare that Major Crombie didn't want any more since his wife had died and there were no other ladies in his family. The tailor from Norwich came over to measure her for a habit, which had been delivered by the carrier on the evening before. On this particular morning I was in the drawing-room, standing on some steps to wash the lustres of the chandelier, a job I never entrusted to anybody; and as the door was open I heard him call to her to go up and try on the habit, and if it was all right they'd go out riding.

'When you say "habit" you mean that long, long skirt, don't you, John?'

'Of course, dear. It came home, didn't it?'

'Yes. But I can't ride in that, can I?'

'Why not. Isn't it all right?'

'I expect so. But I couldn't get my legs over.'

'You won't have to. You'll sit like those ladies we saw at Brighton.'

'I could never.'

'You could learn.'

'They looked like great potato-sacks. I thought they were like that because they were old, or too fat in the leg. I would not wish to look so. If I can ride as I can ride I will and love it. But I will not go wobble, wobble, wobble, and fall off at any moment.'

'You won't fall off. I shall be there to take care of you. Run along, now.'

'Can't I really wear my red skirt and ride so?'

'Darling, do you want to please me?' I smiled to myself at that, it sounded so funny to hear Master John having to coax; we'd all had to coax him.

'I am always pleasing you, John. Nothing have I done all these weeks except please you, please you.'

'Don't you like pleasing me? I try to consult your wishes over a great many things.'

'I know that. But it is only because at the moment it pleased you to. If it made you tired you wouldn't.'

'Now you're talking nonsense. I'm waiting.'

'Oh well, if I must look like a potato-sack I suppose I must.' She went running upstairs.

I thought what an ungrateful little minx, whimpering about pleasing him when he'd quarrelled with his mother over her and thereby cut off his source of supplies and probably upset lots of his friends, for I noticed that the county people hadn't been over-eager about visiting the Manor lately. And I thought of all the nice young ladies who'd have gone on their knees every night and morning with gratitude for a husband like the master. By the time I had finished all these thoughts she came running down again; and she did surely look very nice, with her dark-green habit and the little hat that showed all her glossy curls.

When they came back, I was helping Flossie to hang curtains at the spare-room windows and I heard her say as she came upstairs:

'I am stiff already, and you think I'm a bundle, don't you?' And then she stuck her head out of the window and called to the groom who was just taking the horses round: 'Keep them there a minute,' and a second after, she went flying down the stairs again. Flossie at the window gave a little cry and a snigger and I bent forward to look.

She'd got on the red skirt that she mentioned, an awful thing that I suppose she'd brought from the Great Harry, and no stockings, only a pair of lovely kid slippers with jewels in their heels, that caught the sun as she scrambled up on to the back of Santa, master's big grey horse. The groom called out: 'Sir, sir,' but before the master could get out she had gone across the park in a flash, over the rails like a bird, and was out of sight, while he stood with the perspiration breaking out on his forehead. Then he said: 'Take the mare away, Tom,' and set off walking in the direction she had taken.

In about half an hour they were back, she sitting laughing with her bare feet in the stirrups, he carrying the slippers in his hand and holding the bridle with the other. She had always a slow tired voice, as if her throat was sore or as if she were being very careful of her words and now the slow hoarse voice came up to us again:

'... and I will ride the mare as you say, all back and elbows, so that Major Crombie can say: "Damn fine horsewoman, your wife, Audley," if I can ride Santa like this sometimes.'

'Very well, it's a bargain,' the master said; then lifted her down and stooped to slip on her shoes for her. I thought to myself that when she said that at the moment it pleased him to give in to her, she had spoken the truth, and I wondered what would happen exactly when the time came that he didn't want to please her. Which would win a stand-up argument?

Then, I suppose, the word went round that she was not so bad as had been feared, and really you would not have known from watching her that there was anything so unusual about her. People began to come to the Manor and to invite the master and her out. And with that the trouble began. I believe Lady Rosemary and her sister started it, a kind of set against her; you know how women can be, without ever being rude or ill-mannered – an eyebrow, a tone of voice, a shrug. I've heard her say in a frenzy of rage that the women, except always Miss Isabel, were pigs to her when the gentlemen weren't present. She'd never shed a tear over it though, just blaze out in a temper and say that she would not go to such and such a place. And he would say that it was her imagination, that he'd seen so-and-so speaking sweetly to her, and that the way to get rid of those fancies was to mix with people more and more. Of course, I heard only fragments of their talks, so I never gathered who exactly had offended her or how; I could only use my guessing-cap. In the end of course he would get sulky and speak sharply and they would go off together, or the people in question would arrive and it would all be over for a little time.

Then one night at a ball – and I know this is true because, it being a charity ball, all the gentlemen who had them lent their butlers, so Barber was there and he heard – Lady Rosemary's sister, who had taken it very hard when the master chose his bride elsewhere, said, perhaps as a joke, when Mrs. Audley was standing near her: 'Very powerful smell of ale around here, isn't there?' And Mrs. Audley whipped round and said in her loudest, hoarsest voice:

'If your nose wasn't quite so big, Lady Phyllis, you wouldn't smell quite so much and you'd be a damn sight better-looking.' You can imagine what an upset that caused. The lady insisted upon leaving at once and the master tried to get the mistress to leave too, but she said he'd crazed her to come and, now that that mannerless woman had left, there was no need for her to go. Of course, lots of the men, and some of the ladies, said it was no more than Lady Phyllis deserved, but most of them were shocked. It was a pretty good answer though, because Lady Phyllis has a remarkable hooked nose like the beak of a parrot.

Next day, I must admit, I kept both my eyes and ears open; I was very curious to know how the master had taken this little happening. I heard nothing all day until the afternoon, when I was at the linen-cupboard and he came upstairs to inquire whether she was ready; they were supposed to be driving out to a house several miles away, to spend the evening. He left the door open, so of course I heard everything.

'No, I am not ready. What is more, I shall never be ready to go to any of their houses any more.'

'A very pleasing prospect opens before us, then,' he said, in the nasty dry voice that was like his father's.

'It isn't any good speaking to me like that,' she replied, and I must say that I admired her spirit. 'If she had come to our place, *she'd* have been odd, but no one would have said she smelt. What is more, you say that a lady would have ignored it, and I say that if I had had time to think, I would have pushed her nose so hard that she'd have been married before the end of the year.' I smothered a laugh in a bundle of sheets and almost held my breath, not to miss any of it.

'You might consider my position a little,' he said.

'And you might consider mine. You should have known how your people would behave to me. I couldn't know, could I? I didn't ask you to marry me, did I? If you knew it was to be a choice between your friends and me, you should have chosen them, not have crazed me into marrying you and then turned against me.'

'I've told you forty times today that she is not a friend of mine, and that I shall never accept any invitation for you to any place where she will ever be.'

'I know; but what's the use? She only spoke for them all. They'd all say the same, only they're too smug. You know, John, I've only one life to live; I don't see the sense of making myself unhappy. All that you give me, all this to eat and all these rooms and servants, isn't enough to pay me for being so unhappy.'

I suppose that was the straightest thing that Master John had ever had said to him; and I liked her better than I had ever done. I thought that those were things that not many women would have dared say to a man who had brought them from an out-of-the-way tavern and made them mistress of the Manor.

And I think I must have been thinking so hard that I missed his next speech, for I heard her say:

'Well, I suppose you'll be more unhappy if we don't go than I shall be if we do. I'll be ready in about ten minutes.' He came out of the room all smiles, and I so far forgot the Great Harry as to say, as I hurried to her door and went in in answer to her voice: 'Let me do your hair, madam. I am better at it than Flossie.'

So it was that, when I had lifted her frock over her curls and was straightening up the room, I saw her open the bottom of her wardrobe and take out a bottle and a glass. She poured out what looked to me like brandy, put in a drop of water from the bottle on her washing-stand, and said, smiling her dark smile at me: 'Dutch courage, Agnes; if ever I needed it I do today.'

She put both bottle and glass back into the wardrobe, but there was nothing in the least secret about the action. And I little thought that I had seen an important thing; perhaps it was a little unusual, but what could you expect?

Things settled down after that, and in the late spring we learned that she was going to have a baby. If perhaps the first flush of their love had been a little rubbed by things they said to one another, it all came back now. They were both in the best of spirits and the master wrote to his mother, I think in the hopes that this news would melt her into sending him the allowance that he had been missing rather sadly. Mrs. Audley took no notice, however.

Young Mrs. Audley was a very poor hand with a needle, but she wanted to make all the baby clothes herself; so in the long afternoons she would come and sit by the window in my room and I would help her. She would look at it so seriously and hold it out to me to look at every ten minutes or so, and she took big slow stitches like a little girl with her first sampler. I knew she'd never sewn anything, and thinking of that made me think of the Great Harry and how this baby that we were sewing for was the one that I'd once said unkind things about; I felt sorry that I had ever thought so badly of her and could only comfort myself by thinking that she was only half Winfarthing – she might have good blood in her some way; they had strange visitors sometimes at that inn.

'I do hope it's not a girl,' she said to me one afternoon.

'Well, that's only natural, everybody likes a boy first, especially when it's an old family with a place like this for its heir. But there's plenty of time, you know. I've seen it lots of times; girls seem a disappointment at first, but you get fond of them. Fathers often like them best, in fact.'

'Yes, but I would rather have a boy, for his own sake. Wildness in a boy doesn't matter, they're expected to be a bit wild. But if it's a girl, poor devil!' Hardly any woman uses the word 'devil', even when talking about Satan himself, and the sound of it came oddly from her red lips as she bent with her head over the white work.

'Why do you say that?'

'Well, you've lived at Welland, you know what we're like. That kind of thing goes better in a boy than a girl. Her life would be all pretence.'

'But you aren't like those, not a bit.'

'Oh ... that's what I tell you, pretence. No one will ever know what my life has been like since I came here. I couldn't have borne it, except for ... and of course we love one another; if that ever stopped ... I just shouldn't stay.'

Funny things to say to a housekeeper; but I knew that this was just a time when she needed someone to talk to, and there was no one really.

She had courage too; there were none of those poses that women in her condition put on, fainting in public places and so on. So one afternoon when I found her hanging on to the rail at the top of the stairs, I was really frightened. I loosed her hands and half carried her into her room and laid her on the bed; I let out her corset and held the salts to her nose, and then, as I took the bell-rope in my hand to summon help, she said in a low funny voice:

'Don't call anybody, Agnes, there's a good soul. I shall be quite all right now.'

'You don't know,' I said; 'you're pretty near your time.'

At that she let out one thrilling yell.

'Don't I know it? And isn't that why? Can't you see that I've been trying to get drunk for an hour? Only it went to my knees instead of my head. So I can't forget it. And I'm frightened. I can't face it. I won't.'

'Now, now,' I said. 'Where's the sense in talking so. What did your mother do, and mine? It's the same for you as for everybody else. And you're young and healthy and have lived a good life. Besides, you'll have the very best attention. You mustn't talk like that. And you mustn't give way. Drinking, of all things! What would Master John say?'

'He mustn't know. He thinks I'm brave. But I had to tell somebody. I've been brave so long, all by myself.'

'That's all right,' I said; 'but you mustn't be silly any more. You'd better have a sleeping-draught and keep here for a bit.' I mixed her a powder and took off her shoes and let down her hair, wondering at myself all the time.

The baby was born in September, a girl, and I asked to be let look after it, as I had looked after the master; so they engaged a housekeeper, not a nurse as they had intended, and I went back to the nursery and was out of touch with things again. When the baby was sleeping, though, I used to go down to the kitchen and have a little talk with Flossie, then wander on into the housekeeper's room and discuss what I had heard over a glass of porter. They'd started going out again, I knew that, for she'd come up with the jewels on her neck to say good-night to the baby. And I never noticed anything amiss, so I dismissed the happening of that August afternoon as just the silly action of a frightened woman, facing an ordeal for the first time. But one night Flossie greeted me with:

'Awful row upstairs tonight. They ain't gone to their party. She's gone to bed and he's gone off walking in the rain.'

'What was it about?' And even as I asked, I felt my heart give a little lurch. I was fond of Master John, but if I was to be quite honest I should have to admit that there was something about his wife that made me more than fond of her. She was different, as if, instead of being lower than us all and having to be careful about what she said and did, she was better than us inside and so could afford to be careless.

'Well, but honest, Miss Trudgett, I shouldn't ought to repeat it, and shouldn't to any outside the house, but Barber said she was drunk.'

'You know that's nonsense. I should think Barber was drunk himself.'

'Perhaps he was, and perhaps he weren't,' said Flossie, and I could see that she hated having her story questioned; 'but what I want to know is why does she always have them violet cachous in her bag and under her pillow and in her dressing-table drawer?' And I had noticed the smell of violets a hundred times and never wondered once! I had no heart to go on to the housekeeper. I climbed back to the nursery and had a quiet think all to myself.

But that wasn't the first time and it wasn't the last, the more was the pity, and soon everybody knew. That kind of thing, like fire, won't be hid; and I made up my mind that I'd take the opportunity of having a little talk with her over the baby's bath one day, for the baby had drawn us together, in a way of speaking. But before I plucked up the courage, she came one morning all wrapped in her cloak, with the old short red skirt peeping out under it.

'I expect you'll be surprised, Agnes. I'm going home today.'

'Going where?'

'To Welland. I don't seem to have been a success here, so I'm going home where everything I do won't be noticed and talked about. You'll look after the baby, won't you?'

I said: 'That's foolish talk. If you've been foolish again that's not so serious as some things that have been forgiven and forgotten. You wouldn't think of leaving that now, would you?' And I pointed to the baby, smiling away to itself in the cradle. She pursed her lips and shrugged her shoulders in the odd manner that she had. 'Added to which ...' I was beginning, when suddenly the master came striding into the room.

'Are you going to persist in this idiotic behaviour?' he said, and there was such a cloud on his brow that I knew nothing could make it worse, so I said: 'Now, sir, speak kindly, that might do a bit of good.'

'You can keep a still tongue in your head and enjoy seeing your prophecy come true. You warned me against her.' The mistress looked at me at that, and I'm glad to say that I spoke up and said:

'I didn't know who I was talking about. I know her now, and I know that what has happened now is partly your own fault.'

'Mine! I should like to know how you make that out.'

'You never had any patience with her over the question of going out, did you? You didn't know how poisonous people could be, and you never troubled to find out. And rather than admit to being frightened she took to what she called Dutch courage. If you took her away and began again ...' All this time she was standing looking at the baby with a funny kind of look, not fond or as if she minded leaving it, but with a kind of pitying amusement. But here she turned and said in her hoarse voice, a little gruff:

'Oh, for Heaven's sake spare me that. And spare me your pity. If this hadn't happened something else would. I knew I couldn't do this properly before I started, I knew what would happen, but you weren't satisfied until you'd married me, and you've tried in a thousand ways to alter me, to stop me being myself. Couldn't you see that it was as bad as lopping off my arm or my leg? What was there to do but get drunk, so that I didn't feel it? I wish I was drunk now. Well, I'm going to the right place. I wish ...' And then her manner changed suddenly, and she became distant and somehow great again.

'Good-bye, Agnes, you've been very kind to me, often against your will, I'm afraid. And good-bye, John, I'm sorry it's been so horrid for you. It's all my fault – bad blood, as you'd say of your horses.

Then the master seemed to wake up.

'We must be mad. Do you realize what you're doing? What do you think people will say?'

'That, thank God, won't be my concern any more. I've had two years of that kind of worry, but I end that today.'

'Very nice for you; what about me, may I ask? I'm going to have an enviable time, living here, with my wife running off back to that sty.' His rage fairly choked him. She was not a bit touched or dismayed.

'You are only repeating now what I said to you two years ago; you were so set on having your own way then that you wouldn't listen to me. Now I'm set on mine. You can get rid of me, I suppose. That has been done.'

I think that they had completely forgotten that I was there; and it seemed so dreadful, remembering that they had loved one another so only two years before, that I said:

'You should recollect, madam, that the master risked all that because he loved you. Don't let it end like this.'

'It's no good, Agnes, he's thrown my people up against

me. And they're me; even the foreign woman that he seems to have heard about – they're all in me. I can't help it. Only they have all had the courage to live their lives as seemed good to them; and I'm going to do the same. Love, you say. Simply that two people wanted to go to bed together. You can come and find me if you ever feel like that again. And you can comfort yourself that none of your friends will see me there; you'd never have come if your horse hadn't happened to go lame that day.'

Most of my sympathy now was with the master; she said such unnatural things, and I remembered the brandy, the violet cachous, and the things that the servants said. I went to the cradle, for the baby was beginning to whimper at the sound of all these harsh words. I heard the master say fiercely:

'You shall stay here, by God, and you shall behave yourself.' And in answer to that she gave a wicked little laugh, so unhuman that a little chill ran down my back.

'You think you can stop me? Don't be silly.' The master stood full in front of the door; he was a big man and angry, so angry that in the battle of words he had been worsted; I was afraid that if she pushed past it would become a matter of blows. She stood in front of him, staring him straight in the face, and after a minute, when everything seemed to draw together towards an explosion, he stood aside and she went out with her light quick step. And in the little room there was only me, rocking the crying baby, and the master, glaring at the window with a look of baffled hate on his face, and the rapidly fading scent of violets that had just for that moment outstayed her.

GEORGE TENNANT, GLOBE-TROTTER, TELLS HIS STORY. 'DEAR LADY, THE BRIGHT DAY IS DONE, AND WE ARE FOR THE DARK.'

A.D. 1870

CHAPTER SEVEN

INDIAN DUST-HEAP

I WAS surprised to see a white woman walking alone in that quarter. Although I had not been long in India I had had time to note and to grow accustomed to a certain amount of ceremony about the goings out and the comings in of the 'memsahibs'. The cantonment lay a mile away, and on the road between that collection of shady bungalows and the town one might see lightly garbed women being driven in shining buggies. But I had never seen one alone on foot shopping in the native quarter. It was this that made me spend an idle moment, while I waited at the corner for Smithers, in watching her. She walked slowly, leaning on a stick, and was extremely tall and thin; on her head she wore a rather limp panama hat and she was dressed in a baggy tired-looking coat and skirt of piqué that had once been white, but was now in the revealing sunshine a dirty grey colour. She disappeared in the doorway of a shop and I stood still, waiting for Smithers, who didn't come. So I was still there when she came out carrying now a bumpy little parcel under her free arm.

I am not given to the indiscriminate impulse of chivalry, and yet suddenly I wanted to do something for her, to carry that ridiculous parcel, to offer her my arm. I had no real intention of doing either of these things, but I did take a few wandering steps in her direction. Then round the corner and down the middle of the road came a bullock-cart, just the ordinary bullock-cart drawn by one emaciated animal. As this vehicle drew level with the woman, the driver after the amiable manner of his kind, bent over and twisted the bullock's tail. I averted my eyes – I must admit that I never grew quite hardened either to the bullocks with their dislocated tails or to the gharry ponies' sore shoulders – so my eyes fell instead on the white figure in front of me. I saw it stiffen, and I saw the parcel taken from under her arm and hurled with all the will in the world, and with singularly good aim, straight at the driver's head.

He fell from his precarious perch into the middle of the road, the bullock wandered on for a pace or two, and I took a few rapid steps towards the women. I could not imagine that so arbitrary an act of justice was going to be passed over without further trouble. The driver rose from the ground with a torrent of imprecation pouring from his lips and I was very much relieved to perceive that so far he seemed uninjured in body and spirit; several natives came into the street and joined in the man's chantings. To me doubtless it all looked far more threatening than it really was, for the woman stood perfectly still and then, seizing upon a second when the driver paused for breath, began a speech on her own account.

I did not, unfortunately, understand a word of it, but it was quite long and very emphatic. When one hears an unknown language spoken, one is more sensitive to the tone of the speech, trying perhaps by that means to guess at its import; and the tone of that speech was sheer arrogance. I had had a pretty opportunity of viewing and hearing arrogance of varying kinds since I had landed in India, but never had I heard it more clearly than in the voice of this one shabby lonely-looking woman, who was moreover clearly in the wrong. She finished off by demonstrating very vigorously with her stick exactly what would happen if she ever saw him do it again; then, lowering the stick, she tapped it sharply upon the road in front of her, catching at the same time the toes of one or two bolder spirits who pressed rather closely towards her.

To my surprise and joy the driver climbed up on his cart again, and the crowd in front of her gave way. And then I became aware of the opportunist who had collared the parcel and was making off with it in an opposite direction; I caught his eyes and, taking a coin out of my pocket, held it towards him. The next moment, with the rather clammy parcel in my hand, I was dashing off in pursuit of the woman, with every good reason in the world for doing so.

'Your parcel,' I said as I came up with her. She started at the sound of my voice and stopped; then she turned towards me and I could see that her eyes – bright green they were, too – were brimming with tears.

'Thank you so much. I forgot it,' she said, and held out her hand.

'Won't you let me carry it a little? I'm walking this way.'

Once more she turned to me, this time with an air of surprise, and then, having looked at me for an appreciable instant, said: 'Well, thank you, to the end of the road.'

We fell into step and began walking along together, I stealing covert glances at the face shaded by the old panama. It was a very yellow and fleshless face, with the skin stretched tightly across from cheek-bone to jaw. The queer light eyes were sunken under discoloured lids and prominent brows, and the wide thin mouth was pale against dark skin.

'Do you think that's quite a safe thing to do?' I began.

'I don't know – I've done things rather like it fairly often and shall probably do something of the same kind again.' Her voice was chilling and her words had a ring of rather weary detachment, as if she were discussing the behaviour of a troublesome person for whom she was unfortunately responsible.

'And do you always walk away just like that?' I persisted.

'Generally. Once someone with a lust for blood flung a brick at me. Look.'

She lifted one of her thin hands and thrust away the greying hair over her temple; I could see, even in the double shadow of her hat and hair, the puckered dark line of the scar. She let her hair fall down again and dropped her hand, and I knew by that simple finished gesture that she had once been beautiful. Only a young child or a woman absolutely sure of her effect would have pointed out a disfigurement with that air of calm indifference. The beauty had all been burned and drained away long ago, but I could not remember when any woman, however lovely, had roused such a burning inquisitive interest in me. And with that gesture and the straight glance of her eyes she had even managed to establish that vanished beauty with me for ever.

'Have you lived long in India?' I asked.

'Almost ten years.' She would, it seemed, answer a direct question, but she made no effort to carry on a conversation; she ignored the opening of the inevitable 'And you?' So I offered, in pique:

'I've only just come out.'

'Oh, and how do you find it? Completely revolting, or are you one of those who hear the temple bells and smell the bazaars and never see anything at all?'

'I don't know. I haven't had time to get my bearings. You sound as if you hate it.'

'Hate is far too mild a word. I think that if I could press a button and submerge the whole country I would do it. But you mustn't let me prejudice you. I probably see all its horrors without the compensating drugs of imagining that I bear the white man's burden or of enjoying the society of my betters.'

Even I dared not say 'Why?' to that, her voice was so bitter. The road branched just then and she stopped again, leaning on her stick and holding out her hand for the parcel.

'I turn here. Thank you once more. I hope that you enjoy your stay. I think most people do. Good-bye.'

'Can't I bring it a little farther? I'm in no hurry.'

'I think it would be wiser not to. Thank you.' So there was nothing to do but to hand over the parcel and take my leave. She held out her hand and I took it, getting a queer little thrill from the feel of its frail prominent bones. I was dismissed.

I looked after her as long as I could see her, a tall, stooping figure in unfashionable clothes, walking slowly out of my sight and, I feared, out of my life for ever. The instant that I could see her no more, I turned and at imminent risk of a heat stroke ran back to the corner, where I had waited for Smithers and where he in his turn was now waiting. I wanted to ask straight away whether he had ever seen her or heard of her. But Smithers had come out to show me things, and I felt that he might be more lavish with his knowledge when his weight was off his feet and his hand encircled a cool glass. So I refrained from asking any questions, displayed, I hope, an intelligent interest in all that he showed and told me, and waited with impatience for the evening. It came and at last I had the pleasure of seeing Smithers ensconced in a long chair, with a glass in his hand and a box of his favourite cigarettes beside him. Then I hesitated. How to begin?

'Tell me, have you ever seen a very tall, rather lame woman shopping in that street where I met you today?' I said. He looked at me, with a little smile that crept over his face and was gone, as he said gravely:

'In godless clothes, carrying her own parcels?'

'That fits her, yes. Who is she?'

'If you mean what is she called, I can tell you; she's known as Mrs. Fisher. But I don't think she is that legally. Did she give you one look and did you immediately rush up and beg the privilege of carrying her basket or sack or whatever it was?'

Which ironic question so nearly described what I had wanted to do that I said: 'Well, as a matter of fact I did carry a parcel for her, as far as that corner where the trees begin. It was like this ...' and I told him about the bullock-driver.

Smithers laughed. 'She'll come to a sudden and sticky end some day. White skin isn't quite at the premium it once was. Did she talk to you at all?

'Only the least bit; not nearly as much as I'd have liked. I found her singularly interesting.'

'In which,' said Smithers, 'you are far from being alone. It's a funny thing; once they get the knack of being attractive, they can grill themselves alive as this woman has, pour acid on their faces, put on ten stone of fat, or lose all their teeth, and they seem to be fascinating still.'

'You know her, then?' I asked; and I felt the joy of an explorer reaching his goal.

'In a way. Fisher himself does some work for my paper in his sober intervals. She herself was newspaper news once upon a time. Didn't you ever hear of Lady Victoria Webling? No, I suppose you were at school; it must be fifteen or sixteen years ago. Well, that scarecrow that you saw today is, or was, Lady Victoria Webling. There was a particularly scandalous divorce, and she went off the rails altogether after it. A man I knew then, fellow named Bigham, knew her father and said her mother wasn't much good – came from a pub or something – and this girl was brought up by her father and given too much of her own way. Anyway, she rode for a fall. Oh, there was a time when you couldn't say anything too bad about her; some silly young fool shot himself in her apartment and his family wanted her tried for murder. I dare say I once knew a good many other choice stories, but I've forgotten. Then, when I'd been here about six months, she came down to the office with a message from Fisher. I recognized her, but I didn't say so.'

'Why did she say it would be wiser for me not to go along that road with her? Is Fisher jealous?'

'He may be, but that wasn't why. Oh no, that was because she's a kind of social outcast, a pariah. You see, there was all that behind her; and you can't lose a past like that, wherever you go. In fact, Indian society, so far as I've noticed it, is rather like those stains that make invisible bacteria visible; every little peccadillo becomes a sin. And no one really believes that she's married to Fisher.'

'Is he poor?'

'Hellishly. Clever, you know, in his way. You can't rely on him, though; he may be sober for a week and then drunk for three. That sort.'

'God, what a life for her! I wonder what makes her stick it.'

'Heaven knows; you know what women are. She left Webling, who had made a fortune in his cottonmills and could have given her anything, and she played fast and loose with a number of men after that, if one can believe a quarter of what one hears; then she sticks for ten scorching years on end to a penniless drunken journalist who isn't her equal in any way. It's a mystery.'

'Love,' I said.

'She's forty, and he's a good bit older. I should call it habit.'

My curiosity was spurred rather than allayed by Smithers' account; I racked my brains for some scheme that would provide me with a means of seeing her again. I could think of none and was at last forced to run the risk of Smithers' jeers and ask him for a suggestion. The jeers of course came first. But in the course of time he exhausted his store of wit and then came out with a helpful idea. He gave me a sheaf of papers for Fisher, with the order for a course of articles on the lines of those marked in the papers and a specially emphatic message that he wasn't going to wait this time as he had last. I was anxious not to make my object too obvious, so I asked if this was his usual way of communicating with Fisher. He said yes, generally he sent a message if there was anyone on hand to take it, or else he sent it by post.

'And does he bring the finished stuff?'

'He used to, but I haven't seen him for an age; he sends or posts to me. Sometimes she comes. If you just take these things they'll think you're something to do with the paper; the personal touch you'll have to supply for yourself. And let me warn you, if Mrs. Chivers-Forsdike sees you go in at that gate, you'll never get another decent invitation as long as you're here.'

I imagined that I could bear that with a praiseworthy degree of stoicism; so, making sure of the address, I set off in the cooling evening, aware of a half-tremulous excitement. I wanted to take some flowers, but that desire was undermined by caution. I was particularly anxious not to run the risk of a snubbing – which I felt she would be peculiarly able to administer. But when I hung half-heartedly about the flower-shop I noticed a few thickly bunched clusters of familiar purple violets. I took the miracle of their presence in that hot shop as one more evidence of what wealth can demand and obtain, like strawberries in January, and bought the lot without feeling extravagant, for the simple reason that I did not give myself time to work out what I had paid in English money. And then I set out to walk to the bungalow that Smithers had described.

It stood by itself certainly, but it was definitely in the native quarter, and as I picked my way, wishing I had not walked, I began to wonder what on earth it must seem like to a woman who had had a town house, a country estate, a shooting-lodge in Scotland, and God knows what else in the way of accommodation. The patch of ground in front of it was utterly neglected, a few trees stood like a screen before the actual front of the bungalow, and there was a shallow veranda all round. This was not used and arranged as the verandas to which I had become accustomed were – there were no long cane chairs or little tables, merely a rusted oil-stove, an old bicycle, and the dog. This latter rose up as I reached the end of the path and placed itself before the open door, then, with no superfluous barking, gave tongue to three deep bays and was silent, obviously listening for the voice which at once cried: 'All right, Balder, I'm coming.'

It was her voice, and a second later she stood framed in the open doorway. Balder immediately and politely moved himself to the side and stood with his eyes on her.

'Good evening,' I said, hating myself for feeling so nervous. 'I've brought a message for Mr. Fisher from Mr. Smithers.' I could hear my voice and the flimsy excuse as it would sound in her ears.

'I see; will you come in?'

I went up the remaining step and found myself in a different world. It might have been one of those chintz-filled rose-scented drawing-rooms that look out through French windows on to fresh English grass. True, the chintz in question was faded from repeated washing and there were, I noticed quickly, no flowers. But everything in the room was fresh, cool-coloured, and clean.

'I'm afraid you'll have to give me the message; but I'm quite used to that, so if you'll sit down and tell me exactly what is wanted, I'll see that it is properly repeated.'

So I sat down in one armchair and she took the other and, with her hands folded upon one of its arms, listened attentively while I repeated everything that Smithers had told me, except the bit about not sending in the stuff late; I boggled at that. When I had finished she nodded her head and said: 'Thank you very much; that will be quite all right,' in exactly the way that any woman takes an order for an absent husband. Her manner was so exactly like that of the woman in our village at home who takes in shoes for repairs while her husband at the back taps away at his work that my awe of her was lessened sufficiently for me to say:

'And I saw these, as I was coming along. I thought you might like them.' I thrust out at her the paper containing the violets. A little colour crept into the yellow skin of her prominent cheek-bones as she took the flowers; and looking at me very straightly with her light eyes she said: 'Do you know, I believe that this is the first time that anyone has brought me flowers in all the time I've been here. I don't know how to thank you. I'm afraid I've forgotten all my pretty manners.'

'I'm glad you like them,' I said somewhat awkwardly.

'I adore them. Just their cool faces call to mind the English spring.'

And there the conversation broke down into that silence which all good hostesses and all, even bad, guests dread. In that silence I was conscious of a low hollow coughing that came from behind one of the closed doors at the back of the room. So, I thought, Fisher was at home, but not to be seen; and I remembered that she had not even told the conventional lie about his not being at home. Once more I experienced a profound, though illogical, sense of pity for her. No doubt she had chosen her way of life, but she could not have known what it would cost her. And I realized with what awful ease a reputation is lost, and what a sense of recklessness such a loss bestows. She had no doubt been a spoiled beauty who had made one mistake and then found that the world was not the pleasant playground that she had been brought up to believe it. I sat in that silence and was very sad for her.

After a moment she lifted her face from the flowers and crossed to the white-painted cupboard that had been built into the wall. I watched her take out a tumbler, a bottle of soda-water, and a whisky-bottle; then she turned to me with a rueful expression.

'I was going to offer you a drink, but there isn't a drain. I'm frightfully sorry.'

'No, please don't bother,' I said.

'There's lemon . . .'

'I should like that,' I said, partly to ease a rather uncomfortable situation and partly to prolong this not too successful visit.

She took out another tumbler and a bottle of lemon juice, opened the soda, and poured out two drinks. With one of them in her hand, she sat down again in the chair she had left.

'What made you come here?' she asked, so suddenly that I had only time to tell the truth.

'I wanted to see you again . . . you see, the other day I saw you do something that I should have liked to do myself. I felt as people must have done when they saw martyrs go to the stake for a faith that they themselves secretly believed in. Can you understand that?'

'Except that I was not the martyr. Well now, that was a very honest answer to an impertinent question. In return I will be honest with you. You must forgive me and not mind. We'll say it's because I am so much older than you. It was very nice of you to show your interest by calling and more than nice of you to bring me flowers, but you mustn't come any more – even if you wanted to. You see, the English people here don't have anything to do with us; with me it is actually . . . I think . . . and if . . .'

'Now,' I interrupted her, 'if you're going to mention Mrs. Chivers-Forsdike, I beg of you to refrain.'

'I was, but only to explain what I mean. I don't want you to jeopardize your prospects or anything just be cause you admired my aim! That was it, wasn't it? You may think I exaggerate, but that is only because you haven't been out very long.'

'I've been out long enough to know that I'd rather talk to you than to any person I've met so far. And the beauty of having no prospects is that I can't possibly jeopardize them. So if I may come again . . .'

She lifted her head and gave me another long considering look and then, with a smile that made her seem young all suddenly, said:

'My dear, if you feel like that about it, come by all means. Come tomorrow. Come to supper.'

'No, I didn't mean that I don't want to be a bother to you. I meant . . .' What exactly had I meant?

'Well, I mean it. If you wake up in the same mind tomorrow, come to supper. If you've gained wisdom in the night, don't come, I shan't mind. I'll tell you something though, I cook everything myself . . . I'm cursed with a squeamish stomach. So the fare will be clean though plain, peculiarly plain.'

Well, here was progress. I was content to take my leave now, and very soon did so. I walked home slowly, having quite a lot to think about. Peculiar woman.

Even more peculiar, I thought, when in the middle of the morning a note was brought to me, which had been handed in at the door.

'I'm sorry, wisdom came to me in the night. Don't come. If you could realize what these years have been like you wouldn't put down this *volte-face* to lack of appreciation. You see, just for a moment I forgot several things that make it impossible for me to have friends.'

There was no name and no initial. I wondered if one of the things was Mr. Maurice Fisher. I should have liked just then to have ten minutes' perfectly frank talk with him. But I hadn't finished there. I am not a person of particularly strong will, but I have, what all rather weak people have, a compensating gift of obstinacy. She had certainly not resented my intrusion into her home; I had that to work upon and I had all the time in the world. I asked Smithers about the articles; they were coming in regularly and were good, and that was all the interest I showed for several weeks. I went to the races and out to dinner several times; I talked to

Smithers and his friends and I spent quite a bit of time in the street where I had seen her first. That was wise, for it was there that I saw her again. I joined her in the strip of shadow that ran down the side of the street.

'You haven't gained wisdom, then?' she asked me.

'No,' I said. 'She may be more precious than rubies, but I will have none of her. Let me carry the basket. Why do you carry all your own things like this?'

'I prefer to. And I don't want Balder to get too used to natives coming to the door. I invariably have my reasons for my actions.'

'Even for withdrawing your invitations?'

'Especially for that.'

We laughed together and walked on, with prayers upon my part that we might see only such bullock-carts as were driven by men rendered somnolent by the heat. This time we did not part at the corner nor at the gate at the bottom of her path. Still carrying the basket I followed her into the room. There, lying across the table with his head pillowed on his arms, was the most wretched wreck of mankind that I have ever seen. The shoulders, elbows, and the curve of the bent back might have been those of a skeleton, thinly clad in a shirt of coloured cotton; and the face that he raised as we crossed the threshold was horrible. Paper white, with red circles around the eyes and a week's stubble of black hair on the chin. His nose, like the dying Falstaff's, was 'sharp as a pen', but, alas, he did not 'babble o' green fields'. I stood hesitant, feeling that this intrusion was ill-timed, but Victoria said, in quite a new voice:

'Come in, this is Maurice. Maurice, this is Mr. Smithers's friend, George Tennant.'

'Oh, the latest, is he? The supplanter? Come in, Mr. What's-your-name. Take a good look at me. This is what you'll be like after ten years of it.'

'You're drunk, Maurice,' she said calmly; 'why don't you go and lie down?'

'That's a good idea, from your point of view. I go and lie down in there by myself; and he stays and lies down with you in here, eh? Very good idea, only I shan't do it. You go home to your own woman.' All this was said in a thick blurred voice that was yet indescribably offensive in its tone; more so than in its import – and that was offensive enough.

'I'd better go,' I said, edging towards the door. But she threw out her hand. I thought: 'She's alone with him and afraid,' so I put down my hat and stood still.

'Maurice,' she said sharply, 'you're offending me and a friend of mine, talking like a fool. Pull yourself together at once.'

To my amazement the man stood up, which I should have thought impossible to begin with, and began to cry, weakly, like a child.

'Vicky, Vicky, I'm sorry. I didn't mean anything. But you know what it is, don't you? I'm sorry, Vicky.'

'Yes, dear, that's all right. Now you go and lie down, as I said; and presently I'll bring you a nice cup of tea.'

He went shambling off through the door at the back, his downtrodden slippers flapping off his thin bare feet.

'I'm sorry about that, but it was bound to happen sooner or later. Sit down, I'll make some tea.'

She was gone only a few minutes and came back wheeling a wagon on which shone silver and bright china. She poured tea into one larger cup and went through the door with it; I heard him speak to her in that same little spoiled child whine and her voice answering him. Then she came out and shut the door behind her, settling down to the dispensing and drinking of tea as if nothing unusual had happened.

'You wrote those articles, didn't you?' I began.

'Guilty, but don't tell on me, will you? How did you know?'

'Well – I mean, I rather guessed that he hadn't.'

'Of course not. Poor soul, it's been coming on a long time. Even when he was still working I used to have to go over it all and alter a lot, after he was asleep. He used to write such a mixture of Dante and Edgar Alan Poe; it's much easier to do the whole thing.'

'What's wrong with him exactly?'

'Disappointment chiefly. I'm partly responsible for that, he says, and I rather agree with him. After that, as a natural result, drink and drugs. I'm sorry you should see him like this; he was one of the most charming and intelligent men I've ever met.'

'Are you all right alone with him, like that?'

'Bless you, yes. He wouldn't hurt a fly. Besides, he couldn't now if he wanted to. Poor soul.'

I thought what a queer conversation it was. She was discussing this man, to whom she had devoted ten years of her life, with me, a comparative stranger, as if he had been the gardener. Yet it all seemed so natural, when I wasn't actually reflecting on its queerness, that I thought: 'This was all inevitable, that I should meet her, know her, talk to her like this.'

Presently she called my attention to a photograph that stood on the white cupboard-top.

'My daughter. Do you think she's like me? Say no, for Heaven's sake.'

After careful scrutiny I said: 'I can say that with a clear conscience. She hasn't a look of you at all. Rather a pity. Didn't you want her to be like you?'

'No, I wanted her to be all Webling and respectable; and I do believe you can read people's characters, and therefore to an extent their fortunes, in their faces. I sent home for that last year, when she was fifteen. I was suddenly appalled at the idea that I brought a child into the world, perhaps to make as big a mess of it as I have. It was a great comfort to me to see that jaw, that forehead, that nose, all Webling. Trevor all over again. I was so glad.'

'Can you tell anything from my face?'

'Oh, several things. The outstanding thing about it is inquisitiveness. You want to know all about people, to see them as you'd see them in a tale. It's a kind probing that you subject them to, but it's a probing all the same.'

'Is that all?'

'Oh no, there are many things. Some things I can tell without looking at your face. There's a gift in our family of just knowing things. Once, I should say about four years ago, you had a love-affair, violent and not very lucky. You thought that was the end of that kind of thing for you, but just lately you've begun to think differently.'

'But that is uncanny,' I said. 'How can you tell?'

'I say it's a gift. That's another thing that I hope young Rachel hasn't inherited. It's most disconcerting, because it's so vague and also because you can't do anything about it. I was frightfully in love with Maurice and I'd never been to India, but the day that we sailed, before we went on board, I could see all this; just what the bungalow was like and how it would all end. I ought not to say "see" – that is too clear. It's more like feeling your future with your hands, in the dark.'

'Does it tell you, this feeling, anything about me – in connection with you, I mean?'

'A little. I know. That will pass, my dear.' I was suddenly so abashed, in case the thoughts I had about her were really tangible to her, that I rose quickly and went away.

I continued to stay with Smithers and I continued to visit her. I saw Maurice Fisher on several of these occasions. Just once or twice he seemed to be in a more or less normal state, but usually he was either truculent or tearful. And the more I saw of her life, of its hard work, its loneliness, and the restraint that was demanded when she dealt with that wreck, the more I admired and loved her.

'Why don't you go away from here?' I asked.

'Well, you see, there are a number of papers that know Maurice out here. They believe he exists, they believe he's clever, my field is already ploughed. It would be rather difficult to create those illusions in a new place.'

'And it is necessary for you to go on doing stuff that they believe is his?'

'Yes. At least I have a pittance; not enough for two. And Maurice kept me, in his good days.'

I left the question there, but once or twice it seemed to me that this state of things would soon come to an end. Her perfect patience with him in whatever mood at first impressed and afterwards hurt me. It was too perfect, it was brittle.

'One day,' I said, 'you'll snap.'

'One day I shall. But I know exactly what I shall do then, that's a comfort.'

'What?'

She went through the pantomime of filling and using a syringe; and I thought what a good thing it would be. Fisher was obviously never going to be any good, either to himself or anyone else. The moral aspect didn't concern me, my thought was that she would be free; I'd persuade her to come away with me, on any terms or footing that she cared to dictate. I thought how we would go to all the loveliest places on earth, and she should have marvellous clothes and wipe away the very memory of these lean years. And I loved to think of all these plans, unspoken as yet because of her great understanding – for so I called her unusual gift – and lying between us like a secret.

I was almost content to wait, so sure was I of the happy ending.

Then came an invitation that I could not very well refuse. I actually thought that I'd better go before poor Fisher got his overdose, for I should have some other way of spending my time after that. So I said goodbye to Smithers, promised to be back in a fortnight, and on my way to the station called at the bungalow behind the trees. Balder knew me now and came a dignified pace or two to meet me. Victoria was alone in the sitting-room, dusting. She wore a coloured overall, and the knot of hair on her neck was slipping.

'I'm going away for a little, a fortnight or less. Write to me, will you?'

She nodded.

'How is he?' I next asked, jerking my head towards the bedroom.

'Terrible all night. He's starting to see things. Isn't that awful for him?'

'Awful for you, I should say.'

'Oh, I dunno. I don't see things.' She brushed back her hair and left a dusty mark on her forehead.

'You will write?' I persisted.

'Yes, I promise. I can't promise though that it'll be particularly interesting. I must save all my style for the bolstering up of Maurice's reputation.'

'And don't go knocking anybody about, will you? I shall wonder about you.'

'I can't promise anything in the way of behaviour. I never have done. You'll miss your train, and there won't be another in five minutes' time, you know.'

I laid down the paper on which I had scribbled the address, and took the hand that she held out to me. Her worn yellow face was additionally marked by the ravages of a sleepless night, and the thin flat lips were quite colourless, yet I wanted to kiss her as I had never wanted to kiss anyone, however lovely. But she was looking at me, with just a suspicion of amusement in those bright sunken eyes; amusement – and something else. So I said good-bye quickly and came away.

I waited a week for a letter, cursing in turn the postal service, her dilatoriness, and my own impatience. At the beginning of the second week I went with my host on a two days' camp and saw no post at all. I was a bad guest, for my attention was elsewhere and my nerves were jumpy. When we got back to the house, there were two letters for me. One was in Smithers's familiar copperplate; the other was hers, that erratic hand could belong to no one else. I tore it open feverishly; I thought that her letter might tell me what her lips and eyes would not.

'My dear after two more nights of "seeing things" I've snapped. Not exactly as you thought, poor dear, but then you'll find that your own state of mind isn't what you thought it was. Everybody wondered why I, constitutionally so faithless, have been faithful to Maurice for so long. For a very simple reason he couldn't live without me. So I could hardly let him die, could I? I've enjoyed knowing you very much and I wish you the greatest happiness. I'm so glad you went just then, so there's no chance of your being tangled up in this. The moon through the window is shining on your last gift of flowers. For them and for many other things – my thanks. Good night. V.'

Knowing the worst, but refusing to admit it, I opened Smithers's letter. I did not read it; a few words and phrases leapt out at me: '. . . will be sorry to hear about the Fishers . . . morphia . . . both dead . . . suicide in both cases . . . didn't seem able even to die privately.'

OLD DANIEL BOLLER TELLS
THE STORY OF FREE BEER
AT THE GREAT HARRY

A.D. 1909

CHAPTER EIGHT

FREE BEER

THERE was a rare commotion when we heard that the Old Harry was closing down; and when it was known that a rich woman from London was going to make it into a country house to live in, lots of people was fair savaged; said the magistrates had done it a-purpose, and there was one law for the rich and another for the poor. On the last night at turning-out time young Jim chalked 'Naboth's Vineyard' right across the door, he having a deal of Bible learning through once working for the Vicar. However, closed it was forby the commotion and the chalk, not to mention the letter in the paper, and we had to walk another mile for our beer.

Then when the lady had been seen once or twice somebody got hold of the tale that she was granddaughter to old Squire Audley; and that brought up the yarn about his marrying a girl from that very pub, and how after she'd led him a rare old dance she'd run off and left him. You know how in a quiet place where there ain't much happening people do store up an old tale and do delight to bring it up in later years. She was said to be a widow and rich and to have one of them new motor-cars; still, nobody seemed to really know.

However, the day did come when, going along to the Old Harry, I came upon a great motor-car, all shining with brass, standing aside the road with its lids open and a shover-bloke peering and poking about in its insides. Now, there is a sight to do a man's heart good; all the times when such contraptions go past you, scaring your nag and raising a dust, is paid for when you see a sight the like of that; so I was just about to whip up the old nag and go sweeping past in my turn, with a 'Who's the best man now?' sort of smile on my face, when the lady that was standing by the shover looked around and held up her hand to me. I just stopped as if I'd seen a ghostie, for there, forby the swell clothes and the shiny car and the shover, was old Carrie Winfarthing, the last of the lot, as was shovelled into the ground the winter before last; sorry too we were, for they'd never have closed the Harry while she was alive; she'd have burned the place down sooner. However, there she stood to the life and I knew at once that all them old tales was for once true. You can't deceive a farmer about a family likeness; know too much about stock, we do. So I reined in the old nag and 'Afternoon', I said, touching my hat with my whip.

'Afternoon,' she said, with that silky look that swells can always put on when they want somebody to do something for them, 'do you happen to be going far along this lane?'

'I'm going so far as the Old Harry, to fetch away some barrels what I bought in the sale. If it's a lift you're wanting, you can get in and come so far.'

'Well, what a coincidence!' she said. 'I'm going to that very place myself.' Then she turned to the man and told him to fix the motor if he could and then wait for Master Arnold and bring him along. If he couldn't do it he must go back into the village and hire; they'd got to be back in London that night, she said; then she got into my buggy – very nimble considering her size – and settled down, all silks and furs, alongside of my sack of meal.

'I'm much obliged to you,' she began in a voice that was a little like a blackbird and a lot like a horse's cough. 'Atkins always manages a breakdown when I'm in a particular hurry, and the men went in yesterday, so I must get there this afternoon. I've changed my mind about something.'

'I only hope none of the chaps see you riding in my buggy.'

'Why?' she asked, and looked at me with eyes so like old Carrie's that I felt a kind of trickle down my back.

'Folks round here,' I said, 'take the closing of the old pub very hard. There's a sort of feeling that it's your doing.'

'What foolish nonsense! I happened to read an account of it in the paper – all about its associations with smugglers and so on. I thought it would be an amusing place to buy. Also' – and her haw-haw voice changed a bit – 'I wanted a place out of reach of London and by the sea for my son. His lungs are not strong. One's children are a great anxiety, aren't they?' and she turned that smile on me, like when she wanted a lift – no heart in it.

'They are. I got sons of my own. I always found the strap a good cure for anxiety.'

'You quaint person,' she said, and laughed that empty rippling laugh again. I hate being called names to my face as if I was a child, and that's a habit that some people have. 'You're quite a character' – I've had that said to me more than once. Savaging it is, too.

Very soon the chimneys of the Old Harry poked up over the sand and I remembered all the times that the sight of them had cheered my heart. I made up my mind to get my barrels off the place quick and not take no notice of all the alterations that was going on. The steep bit of sandy slope that went down to the back door was all marked with the wheels of wagons loaded with bricks and stuff, and as we turned on to it we could hear tapping and hammering and the voices of a lot of men.

I reined up and opened the buggy door for her to get out, and then tied my horse's head to the post where I always had done for the last forty years and more.

'Once more, thank you a thousand times. Bless you,' she said in that silly voice, and went tripping off over the sand in her high-heeled shoes that dug in at every step. I was going towards the barn when some man, foreman I suppose, called out, officious: 'Now then, what's your business?'

'My business,' I said, and went on to the barn.

'No one's allowed on here,' he says, coming after me.

'I've come to get something that I couldn't bring home on the night of the sale. Your missus knows all about it,' I said, and went on. Jumped-up young fool.

When I'd got my barrels to my buggy I found that they wouldn't both go in aside my meal and leave room for me to ride. So, as one was to be a meal-barrel, I thought it might as well begin then and I opened the sack and poured the meal into the barrel. While I was doing this the motor-car came sliding up in the sand, and out of it gets her ladyship's son – a lounging discontented-looking customer of about two-and-twenty. She'd apparently seen him arrive, for she called out of an upstairs window:

'Arnold, darling, come and choose the bedroom you'd like.'

'I shan't like any of them. And if I did, you'd only pull it about till it wasn't recognizable.'

'Arnold, how can you? When all I do is for you?' To that he made no reply, but went lounging round the corner of the house, as if he was too tired to stand up. I was just tying the sack over the mouth of the barrel when I heard her voice again, in the kitchen this time.

'What a find! Oh, what fun! We must get everybody in.' And she came to the door, calling, all blackbird this time: 'Croxton, tell the men to stop and come to the door, with their mugs or bottles or whatever they have. And where is the dear soul that gave me a lift? Oh, there you are, not gone; so glad. Come right in.'

I suppose it was curiosity that took me in, for 'dear soul' had savaged me again. I found that the brewer's men in clearing out had overlooked a cask of beer, and this one of them had broached, for her son was in the kitchen with her. The men, obedient to the foreman's whistle, had stopped work and gathered around the door; and then I did see something queer. Madam suddenly turns up her sleeves and, laughing and joking; serves out the beer with her own hands, lily white they was too and all asparkle with jewels. It sounded like old times; and I was only sorry that the poor old man, by which I mean the picture of Harry, whoever he was, was gone and couldn't look down on us no more. And I thought what a funny thing blood was; she annoyed me like mad when she was all fluffy and silly, but now, with a decent job in hand, she was as tidy a piece as you could wish to see. And thinking of that, I heard that young cub say what I thought was cheek, coming from him:

'It's a pity you can't always serve beer, darling, it suits your style. We ought to drop the Webling-Cartwright and get the licence back. It'd be better than turning a decent pub into a blasted "Four Winds" or something!'

A SILLY LADY TELLS A SAD STORY A.D. 1918

CHAPTER NINE

NO LOVE

It is very lonely in this nursing home. And this morning the doctors told me that there is no hope of my ever leaving it until I go out to the cemetery. I am not exactly sad about that; after she is forty a woman lives, consciously or not, in the lives of her children or in the lives of her friends, so that even in the best of health and out of this place I should perforce still be lonely. For I have no friends left and the child is gone – to safe keeping, they assure me. Today the sun is beating down on the white road that runs along under the poplar trees, and the air is full of the songs of birds. I wonder sometimes if we have more than our share of birds this spring, if all those whose haunts are now raked with shell-fire and noisy with bullets have come here to share with me the exile and solitude of this place. I feel that for me life ended a long time ago; and to keep my mind from dwelling on the past bitterly I am going to write down as accurately and fairly as I can this story of an adventure, experiment, infatuation – call it what you will. No one will disturb me, for I see no one; and that doesn't make me sad either, for the only person that I want to see wouldn't want to see me. . . . Besides, I think he is dead. For when after the inquiries which it seemed *I* had no right to make I found that Arnold was a prisoner, I knew that he must be dead. His was not the nature to endure even the mildest form of captivity.

I look at that sentence with all the knowledge of him

that it implies, and think, if only I had known it sooner! It was in England that I met Arnold first. I had been ill and my husband had insisted upon my leaving Constantinople before the summer came. I was staying with my sister in Norfolk and one day we went to call upon a neighbour of hers, a Mrs. Cartwright who had a house by the sea. We found the woman in a state of suppressed excitement; apparently her son, who had been away for a year in Africa, had come home unexpectedly. She could talk of nothing else but her surprise and joy at seeing him again, and all together it was a very boring hour with both my sister and me fidgeting to get away; she insisted, however, that we stay for tea, and so I met Arnold. It is strange to think that, had she been a trifle more boring and a trifle less pressing, all that happened later would have happened to some other woman, not to me. At least I think so.

At first sight, I think, Arnold was rather a disappointment. His mother's talk had prepared me for a Colossus, an Adonis, and all we saw was a slight lounging youngish man, who drifted in with a dog at his heels and gave us all a bored and casual greeting. I have always suffered from a peculiar kind of shyness which forbids me to look at or talk to any person who does not appear to be definitely and personally interested in me; so it was not until we were leaving that I really looked Arnold Cartwright in the face, and it was from that moment that he took complete possession of my imagination. Only of my imagination, I would point out; for I was at that time, and for six months after my return to Constantinople, perfectly faithful to Ian in body and as faithful as I could possibly be in mind.

It was not long before Arnold and I were meeting every day, somehow. Many of our meetings were public; and my sister laughed at me for having tamed 'the wild man', as she called him, while his mother seemed to welcome anything that would keep her darling with her a little longer. She was devoted to him in a fussy uncertain irritating way that was a little pathetic in so imposing a woman.

The summer went very quickly and there came the afternoon when I had to tell Arnold that I was leaving at the end of the next week. He took the news very badly and I regretted not having deferred it until the day before I left. We parted before dinner in a miserable mood and I spent a wretched evening, longing to go over to his house just to see him. But prudence spoke at that moment with a louder voice than love, and I went eventually to bed, unhappily enough.

Arnold came to me that night; and it is not an encounter that I care to think about even now. He was horribly outspoken, tried to persuade me to let him in – he was on the balcony then, and raved about life being so short and the criminal folly of wasting a minute or an experience that we might yet have together. And the part that I hate to recall is the fact that I was tempted so much that another word might have prevailed against me. I mean that, short of the final and actual surrender, I did commit adultery with Arnold that night. And from that night a kind of decay set in. I began to regret my scruples and my upbringing, which kept me away from what I wanted; and I began to hate the idea of going back to Ian. Even his face, which seemed to look at me with reproach from the photograph beside my bed, roused in me a wild impatience and I turned it to the wall.

Next morning I rose at six, packed feverishly, and after a hasty and not too satisfactory farewell to my sister I left for London, giving some urgent shopping as my excuse. At the end of the week I left for Constantinople. I had neither heard from nor made any sign to Arnold.

Ian was pleased to see me and we seemed at once to plunge into the round of social duties and pleasures that constituted half Ian's 'work' and all my life. I was very unhappy and realized that men were quite right to despise women, as secretly they do; in an emotional situation women lose all dignity and all sense of proportion. I, living exactly as I had done before that fateful visit, was now unhappy where I had been very happy, simply because I was haunted by a lean brown face set with eyes of a peculiar light grey. And that face belonged to a man about whom I knew really nothing, merely that he had caused his mother a great deal of anxiety without giving her much consideration; that he was a wanderer, an extravagant spender of money that he had not earned, and a somewhat impetuous lover.

All these thoughts and feelings I had of course to conceal, and the time came when I began to think that this concealment, added to my unrest, was affecting my nerves. I imagined that I was being followed and watched by some invisible spy. One night as I sat in my room and leaned my arm on my dressing-table and my head on my arm I felt rather than heard a movement behind me. The curtains were drawn over the open windows, and as I turned sharply that way, I noticed that they were all stirring – in the wind, I thought. Yet something drew me towards them and I laid my hand on the velvet and pushed it very softly aside. As I did so I had a vision of a pale wild face, which had no sooner fallen on my sight than it had vanished. It was Arnold's face, and I knew then that my nerves had gone and that I was 'seeing things'.

Two nights after that, there was a ball at the Embassy. I dressed for it languidly; the satin and the diamonds seemed like the trappings of a corpse, so hollow and empty was I.

Soon after midnight a footman came to me and in a low hurried voice, with some apologies, confessed himself unable to dispose of a stranger who had demanded to see me and who said that if he were sent away without seeing me neither the footman nor himself would ever be forgiven by me. 'I will come,' I said; and as the man opened a door I found myself face to face with Arnold. 'All right,' I said to the attendant, and pushed the door to behind me. I meant to be calm and cool, to profess surprise at seeing him; but the moment the door clicked we were in one another's arms and resolutions were less than smoke wreaths.

When we looked at each other we were both breathless.

'What are you doing here, Arnold?' I asked.

'Just going through, you know, and thought I'd like to see you.'

'Going through? Where?'

'I'll tell you presently. How have you been getting on without me?'

'Very well,' I said. Then I remembered. 'When did you come? Did you look in at my window two nights ago?'

He laughed. 'I've been here just over a fortnight. I've seen you lots of times. But I don't suppose I'll see you any more, unless . . .'

'Unless what?'

'Unless you like to up stick and come with me. Stop! I'll tell you all the disadvantages first. I've hardly any money and I shan't be getting any more from the old source. Secondly, you'll have to break those precious marriage vows that you rate so highly; and forget them too, no remorse. But there are things in its favour. I'm going to a heavenly place, where we'd be free as few people are. We'd be what all lovers long to be, absolutely by ourselves.'

'Oh,' I said, 'this all sounds very engaging. Would you mind telling me where it is?'

'It's an island, away down in the South Seas. There's only one white man on the island; he's a Greek who keeps a sort of store. Another one is down there loading a boat of stuff to take to him now; he goes once a year. He's going early tomorrow morning, and I'm going with him.'

'But why?' I said.

'I dunno. Just fancy, I suppose, and it sounds marvellous; the question is, will you come too? Think of a green island set in the sea, with a view, perhaps, of others just smudged on the skyline. Imagine the quiet and the great trees. Lovely, don't you think?'

'Lovely enough, but you know very well that I can't go rushing around the world in search of loveliness.'

'Why not?'

'I told you, I have Ian to think of. I have duties and responsibilities. I have a conscience.'

'Well, may your conscience and your thought of duty well done comfort you when you lie a-dying, knowing that you gave up something you wanted because of them.'

'That's a cruel thing to say. I don't think you realize what you're asking me to do.'

'Perhaps not. Anyway, you're going to stay here, aren't you? Very well, you shan't say I persuaded you to do anything against your will. We leave at six. If you should change your mind before a quarter to, you'll find me at the end of your street. But you'd better say good-bye rather nicely to me now, because at six o'clock you'll be in your virtuous bed, sleeping the sleep of the just.'

He pulled me towards him and kissed me again; and although I would not kiss him, and although the casual way in which he had made his proposal rankled in me, the touch of his hands through the thin satin of my dress, and the pressure of his mouth on mine, turned my heart to water. When he let me go, I was shaking, and I waited in the little room for some minutes after he had torn open the door and gone. At last I was calm enough to return to the ball-room and find Ian; pleading a devastating headache – a thing I was rather prone to having – I went home. It was almost one o'clock.

My maid was waiting. I sent her away and locked my door. Then I sat down on my bed and tried to think. My mind veered like a weathercock. At one moment I was so determined that I was staying with Ian that the idea of doing anything other than that seemed like the wild imagination of a nightmare. The next saw me drag out a suitcase and begin to fill it with fingers that shook with haste. I heard Ian pause at my door on the way to his room. He did not try the door. I thought of the many ways in which he had been kind and generous to me and I unpacked everything again.

And at last it was five o'clock. I had reached no decision. I felt the minutes of that hour slip through my fingers as if they had had an actual substance; my blood as it raced round my body and throbbed in my temples cried: 'Hurry, hurry, make up your mind!' At a quarter past five I let my dress slide off me to the floor and laid the diamonds on the dressing-table. I had exactly twenty-five minutes in which to write something to Ian, to collect all the things that I should need, and to join Arnold in the road outside. I did it of course. The last thing to attract my attention was the travelling-clock which was a dear possession and which always stood beside my bed. I snatched it up, wondering as I did so whether it would be the only timepiece in the place to which we were going.

Arnold had not waited a fraction of a second, he had already turned the corner and was walking away from me when I reached the end of the road; but my agony of indecision was ended, the sight of his back disappearing in the greyness made me run madly in pursuit. I called: 'Arnold, Arnold!' at the top of my voice; he heard me, started, turned, and dropping the bag he was carrying, ran back to me and caught me in his arms. I let my bag drop into the mud of the roadway and for some minutes we stood locked together. The thought of the time made us jump apart and we seized our bags and ran panting and laughing towards the shipping.

It was so that the experiment began.

It wasn't a success!

Palica was as beautiful as any earthly place could be. We lived in a house that the Greek storekeeper had built for himself and then abandoned because it was too far from the beach. It stood, clustered with trees and buried in flowering creeper, by the side of the stream that went gurgling past.

The natives were like friendly happy children, and the sunshine was a perpetual benediction; there was every prospect of our money and clothing lasting for ever. It is very hard for me to describe the atmosphere of a place where neither wealth nor clothing nor social ambition plays any part.

For a long time – I suppose, looking back, it was for two years or a little more – we were blissfully happy. We lay in the sun and talked and made love to each other, we experimented with native foods, we bathed and fished. It must have been two years, because I remember that twice the old Greek Captain came and that I endured agonies until he had gone again lest Arnold should take as sudden a fancy for leaving Palica as he had for coming to it. But although he was pleased to see the man and spent the greater parts of several days and nights in drinking and talking with him, he showed no inclination to go back.

He was frequently drunk in the first two years. There was always whisky to be had at the store, and, failing that, there was a potent native brew, the mere thought of which made me shudder, for I had seen the young girls whose job it was, preparing the substance of which it was made by chewing it to a certain fineness and then spitting it out into the bowls. This process for some reason did not disgust Arnold in the least. It seems a small thing, but I believe that it was the sight of him calmly drinking this stuff that first laid a film of disenchantment over my adoration for him. It was so very unfastidious; I would watch him and think of their chewing mouths, the drip of the saliva, and the noise of spitting, until every mouthful that he swallowed gave me a feeling of nausea, and I would put off the moment when he would kiss me by childish excuses.

Then, too, the natives, although they had the outlook and natures of children, had some peculiarly revolting customs, particularly in connection with their marriage ceremonies. Once Arnold went to see a native wedding, and returned in a frame of mind that I can only describe as sadistic. I was very fond of him – he could rouse me mentally with a word, physically with a touch – but there is nothing of the masochist in me. That night was probably a revelation to us both.

Environment is a curious thing, and I suppose many things which would have been signs and warnings to me in a civilized community passed me by here, where the senses were lulled by the everlasting peace and beauty. Or it may be that the languor that rots people who are transplanted out of a temperature into a warm climate had had its effect upon me. Arnold went on one long fishing expedition after another, and it was not until I saw a brown girl nursing a remarkably pale baby that suspicion shot through me. Even then I wondered. The Greek at the store had no wife and I had seen native women going in and out of his house. The pale baby might be his. I made up my mind to ask Arnold, but I put it off from day to day and somehow I never did.

That year, when the trading ship came, the Captain came to see me and offered to give me a passage. I was astounded. I asked the reason for his offer. He said that he was sorry for me and knew Arnold would never leave now. Nor would he live long, he thought, judging by the look of him. That shook me. Arnold and I might be out of sympathy, but I loved him. So much, I realized, that I was willing to forget the half-caste baby, since to mention it might shatter the calm of our relationship. I did not want him to stay here if it was going to kill him; better go back where we were known, even if it meant dire poverty and ostracism. I told the trader that I would talk to Arnold.

'But you won't come away quietly by yourself?' he asked.

'No, why should I?' I said. I think he thought that I was weak in the head, for with a look of pity he put down the bundle of English and American magazines that he never failed to bring me, and stumped away. Arnold was drunk when he came back, but that was nothing new and I let the discussion wait till the morning. I began by saying that the Captain had offered us passages.

'Oh, so you've had enough of it, have you?' he said unpleasantly.

'No; I was thinking of you.'

'What about me?

'He thinks the life doesn't suit you – that you're not looking well.'

'I'm perfectly all right, as he'll see if he doesn't mind his own business. I'd look a damn sight worse if I got anywhere within reach of the police, I may tell you.'

'What do you mean?'

'Never mind that. It's over. Besides, I like it here. But you go if you like.'

The casual permission woke in me the despair that I had felt when in that hurried packing I had heard the clock strike and feared that he would go without me after all. But I was stung as well as hurt, and said acidly: 'I know that you could manage very well without me. I expect that Tia would enjoy living here.'

And Arnold of course laughed.

'So you knew about Tia, did you?'

'Yes,' I said, and I was horribly conscious of the futility of any discussion between us two. 'I suppose everybody on the island has had the laugh on me, but I don't care.'

'They don't think like that. You see, they're only poor savages; they only see things with natural eyes.'

'As you do, I suppose?'

'Exactly,' said Arnold. 'Well, what are you going to do about it?'

'Nothing.'

'Good girl,' said Arnold.

So we stayed on and began our fourth year. And although Arnold was certainly pale and heavy-eyed and often cross and liverish, he was never definitely ill. So I forgot the Captain and Tia and the fact that he had never told me what it was that the police were after him for. That didn't seem to be a real thing at all. Nothing was real except the little house under the trees and the lazy unreal life.

Tia was not the only one.

And then Esther was born. I suppose few English babies have ever been born in such strange circumstances. No doctor, no nurse, no long white robes or feeding-bottles or woollies knitted by adoring grandmothers. But for almost four years I had lived a life so like a native woman that the modified native treatment sufficed, and Esther was as lively and healthy a baby as you would find anywhere. With her coming, however, something that I suppose people would call the maternal instinct arose in me. I made up my mind to leave Palica the next time the Captain came. Arnold might stay. Perhaps for the first time I saw him as he really was when I considered him as Esther's father. I thought what her life would be if we stayed there. She would grow up wild and untaught, playing games with her half-brothers, Tia's little boys – there were two now – and with the little girl who had Arnold's queer light eyes. Her mother was the most beautiful girl in Palica, yet nobody thought it queer that she should have dealings with the drunken white man; Arnold had found his way to the very heart of the natives.

That year the Greek did not come with the stores. We watched and watched, but the sky-line was never broken. Arnold mocked at me and said that even the stars in their courses fought for him. I knew a very sickness of despair. I thought of all that I had read of another island, where some English people settled long ago in Napoleonic times, and how they had been forgotten there and left to live their savage lives, degenerating with every passing year. I imagined Esther growing up and marrying a native, perhaps going through that awful wedding ceremony. I saw the wicked fool I'd been, renouncing my obligations to Ian, to my generation and my race, and now, worst of all, to this poor dependent little thing. Imagine the position for yourself. I tried to make up my mind to kill her; then I thought that while there was life there was hope, someone might come; I thought too that the natives were happy, and perhaps that life as a native was better than no life at all. Besides, she was such a sweet baby.

The Greek did not come in the next year; that was 1916, and we had been on the island for a little over five years. Then suddenly a quite different ship appeared on the horizon and came towards the island, where we stood rooted to the beach. It stopped outside the reef, and we held our breath lest it should think us unworthy of a visit and pass on. But we saw boats being lowered, filled with sailors – American, the Greek said. They came in and the boats grounded on the beach. Then for some minutes all was confusion and the chattering of excited people. It was, as the Greek said, an American ship, in need of fresh water. The stream, said the Greek, was fresh and pure, and he began, still chattering, to lead the way. There had been no ship, no ship at all he assured them, near the island since 1913.

'Then you haven't heard that there's a war on,' someone cried incredulously.

'A war! You don't mean England and France, do you?' That was Arnold's voice. He had come through the trees in time to catch the last words.

'Sure, England and France all right, but they're on the same side. Russia's with them against Germany and Austria. Say, that's odd. Imagine there being a place where that wasn't known and the whole world thinking of nothing else!'

'God,' said Arnold, 'and are you folks in it?'

'Not yet,' said the sailor significantly. 'You're English, ain't you?'

'What did you think?' asked Arnold impatiently. He was white beneath the dirty tan and stubble on his face, and the words came from him in jerks. 'How're they getting on? Man, don't you know anything about it except that the whole world knew and I didn't?'

The sailor looked at him with slightly contemptuous surprise. His appearance, like my own, was little calculated to command respect or attention; and I suppose the sailor did not expect to find a burning English patriot lurking in Palica. But Arnold laid his hand on the man's elbow and drew him off the path, into the shade of some palms. They fell at once into an earnest conversation. I hurried up to our house. I was determined to leave on that ship if it were in any way possible. If I had ever prayed for Esther's future welfare I should have regarded this as an answer; but of course I had never done so. I now put my clock and a few other things, very few, into my suitcase. Then I washed the baby and myself, fed her, and cooked a simple meal, which I was eating standing up when Arnold rushed in. He stopped at the sight of me standing by my case and said: 'How did you know?'

'What?'

'That I'd persuaded the Captain to take us on. It's irregular, he says, but then, I must get back.'

'Why?' I said.

'Didn't you hear? England's at war, with her back to

the wall too. They're talking about conscription. Kitchener's dead. Where did my razor get put to?' He shot these remarks at me while he searched round the room. I blew on the ashes and made enough fire to heat him some water, and he shaved himself with hands that trembled more than usual. The sight of them made me say: 'Do you think you're fighting fit?'

'I shall be by the time we make England. Anyway, they can't afford to be fussy, so that fellow said. I wonder where they'll drop us and how soon we'll be there.'

And that was how the adventure ended. Palica and all that it had meant sank into the blue water in the dazzling light of the afternoon. And it seemed as if London rose up, grey and dirty, in its place. I was like someone walking in a dream, enduring many things without the power to arrange or alter or prevent anything. When Arnold tried to make some financial arrangements for me I could have cried with relief, yet some nightmare perversity made me say:

'There's no need for you to bother; I am perfectly able to look after myself.'

'And the baby?'

'Of course I can look after her. It's the privilege of the unmarried mother, isn't it?'

'There's no call to be bitter,' said Arnold.

And that was how most of our discussions ended, for he was too much absorbed in his own immediate plans really to trouble about anything else; and I was ancient history anyway. Once I asked him about his reason for not coming back before; was it safe now? With a peculiar smile that told me he had invented the whole story, he said it was perfectly safe. Somehow, despite the hands that trembled and the cough that nothing would quite cure, he scrambled into the army and I was left with a small child, twenty-four pounds, and my two hands to face life in war-time London. There were those who would willingly have given me a secret kind of charity for the sake of old times; I knew that, because I have many times been surprised at the shabby pensioners who depend entirely upon the goodwill of some flighty society woman whose heart might have been judged to be as hard as her diamonds. But that kind of charity was not for me.

It is getting dark in this room, the nurse will come soon. I have been writing all day and am now no clearer in my mind. The times that followed, the train of circumstances that brought me first to driving a lorry in France and then into a French nursing home, to die of some germ in my spine that nobody seems to know anything about, had no connection with Arnold. If he lives and cares to do so he can take Esther out of the covent orphanage; if he is dead, as I think he is, she will be safe for a time at least. I shall not see either of them again. It is quite dark now, I can hardly see the paper. I have occupied myself today and I must think of something for tomorrow, if I should happen to wake again.

JANE ARGENT TELLS THE STORY OF THE CHINESE FINALE

A.D. 1935

CHAPTER TEN

CHINESE FINALE

'I GREATLY regret that I have no Society doctor to send to Pi Lung,' wrote the Society's secretary-in-charge in response to our fifth appeal; 'but there is a sad dearth of labourers in this department. However, I have heard of an English girl who, my friend assures me, is very anxious to work in some pioneer station. I should not of course think of appointing her without some probation, or indeed at all, under more usual conditions; but I do feel that with things as they are we are unlikely to find a more orthodox candidate, and that in view of the coming winter and Mrs. Pether's confinement, it is urgent that you have medical skill at hand. The girl is young, but has exceptional ability, I believe, and we must hope for the best. Should she decide to accept our offer, she should be with you by the 15th or 16th at latest. What horrible news from Koncha! ...'

Well, we in Pi Lung were several hundreds of miles nearer the scene of the Koncha atrocities than the secretary, so we thought as little about them as we could and read and re-read the part that told us about our new colleague. Mrs. Pether was still referred to as our latest addition, although she had been with us for four years; so you may imagine with what excitement we awaited the arrival of the new doctor. Having been without a doctor for six months and with Mrs. Pether daily before our eyes, we were so pleased and relieved by the secretary's news that we were strongly prejudiced in her favour before ever we saw her

First appearances are frequently misleading. We remembered this and agreed not to be disappointed when we had welcomed Dr. Cartwright and passed the hours after supper in her company. All the same, she was not what we had expected or hoped for. After all, we were, first and foremost, a missionary settlement. By common consent not one of the four of us had ever cut off our hair, smoked a cigarette, or used stronger language than 'bother' or 'drat'. Dr. Cartwright seemed to smoke incessantly and we lost count of the times she swore in those two hours. I admit that she had some cause for annoyance; it appeared that the convoy had lost some of her medical stores on the journey up, but that did not seem to excuse the use of the expression 'b— Chinks' of the poor lost souls amongst whom she had come to labour. She contended of course that the things had been stolen. She used the word 'heathen', too, as a term of reproach, and I could not refrain from thinking that to a decent Christian woman her own appearance more than merited the epithet. She had reddish hair, very short, and what there was of it was pushed back anyhow behind her ears. Miss Andrews, our chief, always made a special point of neatness of appearance, and I caught here eyeing Dr. Cartwright rather sharply once or twice. I wondered what she thought of the old stained scratched leather coat with its zip fastener bulging at the front and the draggle-tail tweed skirt. I even wondered whether amongst our young charges she would pass for English, for her skin was a dirty yellowish colour and she had pale flat lips.

She was very little comfort to women who had for a long time been exiled from their native land and from civilization; she told us none of the little chatty things with which Mrs. Pether had entertained us during her first month or so. She had come from England only a few months before, yet when Mrs. Pether asked what the fashions were really like in London, she made no attempt to think up an answer, but merely said in her odd gruff voice:

'I'm sorry, I've no idea. That kind of thing doesn't interest me at all.'

Unnecessarily rude, I thought. And yet perhaps she was not unkindly disposed towards us, for after supper, while she was unpacking what seemed to be her only suitcase, she came into the sitting-room with a huge sheaf of papers which she flung on to the sofa.

'I thought you might care to see these. None very new, I'm afraid; the mails weren't through when I left.' Unfortunately they were none of them papers likely to appeal to godly women, but *Spectators, Bystanders,* one or two copies of *Punch,* which is a clean paper I admit, and six or seven of a disgusting thing called the *Keyhole*. Miss Andrews got hold of one of the last-named; I saw her frown and then she called me.

'Am I dreaming,' she said, 'or does this really mean what I think it must. How utterly appalling!' She made as if to throw it into the stove, but I said:

'Better give it back to Dr. Cartwright, don't you think? It's her property, after all.'

'You may be right, Miss Argent,' she said. 'I will give them to her in the morning; it may afford me an opportunity to tell her what kind of thing is in good repute here.' Mrs. Pether, dear soul, tried as always to smooth over any little annoyance and said:

'She may have heard what a rake Arthur is and tried to suit his supposed tastes.'

Everybody looked affectionately at Arthur Pether, who since Dr. Lorkins's going had been our only man and something of a mascot; and the cloud passed from Miss Andrews' brow.

The social weather at the Pi Lung station depended almost entirely upon Miss Andrews, who was a warm-hearted and high-principled woman, but utterly illogical and prone to be prejudiced. I had seen two capable and popular assistants leave, in what was tantamount to disgrace in one case and dudgeon in the other, simply through not being able to agree with her. I was therefore greatly relieved to observe Dr. Cartwright come in with the chief for the midday meal, talking and occasionally laughing. Before the meal was over, however, they had fallen out over some woman who had been at the clinic that morning. I am afraid that I shall tell this part of my story badly, for I know nothing of medicine beyond a few rather grandmotherly cures for chilblains and colds and so on, and medical terms always sound terribly horticultural to me. Still, I know cancer when I hear it, and I heard it that day mentioned sharply several times, in a heated conversation at the top of the table.

'... nothing could possibly do her any good; I don't suppose for a moment that the most skilled surgeon in London would do more than make sure that the end was as painless as possible.'

'I don't agree with you. That woman is one of our most promising converts, she has a large family. It would be a great thing if our treatment under the hand of God could cure her, as I believe it could. In fact, I shall be greatly distressed if we revert to a defeatist policy and the use of palliative drugs.'

I admit that the chief flung these words over the table with a definite challenge, but it was too sharply taken up.

'Obviously cancer doesn't mean to you what it does to me, or you wouldn't speak like that about palliative drugs. If you'd ever seen a case get beyond their help you'd probably speak of them with a little more respect. As for the woman being a convert, unless something is done to relieve the pain, she'll be in a condition to get converted to anything you care to mention; she'll be stark crazy.' Dr. Cartwright bent determinedly over her plate, cut her meat across two or three times, and then, as if aware that Miss Andrews had fixed her with a very angry eye, looked up and laid down her knife.

'You were aware, I suppose, that Pi Lung was a missionary station?'

'Certainly. And I knew that it was an outpost. That made me keen on it. I was desperate for a job anyhow. But I never pretended that I had any missionary zeal. I even told that secretary person that I'd never attended a Church of England service in my life. I'm afraid you'll just have to use me and ignore any views that offend you. And we'll not discuss things at table.'

And that no doubt was meant to be an amicable and placating speech. But Miss Andrews was not in the habit of being told what to discuss and what not to discuss at what she regarded as her own table. She went on with her food in an offended silence and the rest of us talked rather tentatively amongst ourselves, studiously refraining from addressing Dr. Cartwright; to have done so would have insulted Miss Andrews and greatly prolonged the quarrel. Recounted like this, it all sounds very trivial, but it was quite real and oppressive at the time.

Dr. Cartwright did not appear at the evening meal, and next day she and Arthur Pether rode to an outlying village at the foot of the hills and so were absent all day. By the second morning at breakfast the tiff appeared to have blown over. We were all glad, for it was easy to see that both the women concerned were of an inflammable nature, and we were not anxious to be left without a doctor again.

Work on the medical side had suffered during the interval between Dr. Lorkins's going and this girl's arrival, and it became a usual thing for Dr. Cartwright to ask me for a few sandwiches and stay at the clinic all day. I never understood how she managed with the smattering of the language that was all she possessed, but she seemed to do very well. Miss Andrews admitted that and said frequently that she was clever and energetic enough, but that it was a great pity that she could not experience a change of heart, because a doctor had such influence on ignorant people.

Conversation, at supper especially, became rather a perilous business. Once, I remember, we rather unusually mentioned the atrocities said to have been committed against the prisoners taken by the notorious revolutionary leader called Tonga.

'Still,' said Miss Andrews, who was a notorious champion of the natives, 'that is no worse than the things which the Germans did to our men.' I am afraid that, living as we did so far from the sources of new thought, we were inclined still to think anti-Hunnishly. Dr. Cartwright looked up and said quietly, with the grin that seemed to be her nearest approach to a smile:

'That's all nonsense, you know.'

'I beg your pardon?'

'I mean that it's generally agreed, in an England where a number of the men were actually in German prison camps during the war, that the Germans did the best they could in the rather awful circumstances.'

'I should want proof of that.'

'You can have it. My own father was captured, latish in the war, after the food problem became urgent. He said that although the food was dreadful – in fact, it is supposed to have started the illness of which he died – it was little if any worse than the food that German civilians were working and paying for and that little children were eating. It surprises me that, considering it was England's blockade, they gave them anything at all. What is more, my father was a very troublesome prisoner. He made no less than three attempts to escape; from two of them he was taken back, but he was only moved to safer camps each time, he wasn't specially starved or knocked about or anything. And lots of fellows would tell you the same.'

'Did he get away the third time?' Arthur Pether asked the question.

'Yes, he got out in time for the last six months.'

'That may be so, although I am not convinced,' said Miss Andrews, ignoring the interruption. 'What I fail to understand is that you seem so tolerant of Germans, for instance, and yet so intolerant of the poor ignorant Chinese.'

'Well, if you want to know why, you've said it. They are so ignorant, and it's not a new country. They were a nation long before the Germans were. But they're ignorant and dirty, a thing you couldn't say about the Germans, could you?'

'The Chinese have their virtues, remember. They are extraordinarily energetic, at least in these parts.'

'Good Lord, energy isn't a virtue, is it? It's a physical state. Look at a bug!'

'When what began as a serious discussion becomes a mere bandying of terms, it is time it ceased,' Miss Andrews said. Dr. Cartwright shrugged her shoulders and rose from the table, fishing a cigarette-case out of her pocket as she did so. I had seen Miss Andrews crossed in argument before and was not surprised to see the light of battle dawn in her eyes.

'I've been meaning to ask you, Dr. Cartwright, if you would very much mind not smoking in the rooms that we all use. In your own room of course, and in the clinic, if you don't mind setting a bad example ...'

'Has it taken you all this time to muster sufficient nerve to say that? Who minds, anyway?' She raked us over with her pale eyes, and we all of us began to mumble that we didn't mind, but the chief seemed to collect all our wavering eyes and all our uncertain voices as she said:

'*I* mind. And that should suffice.'

There was the suspicion of a grin on Dr. Cartwright's face, but she went out without a word; we who had had no part in the quarrel sat feeling small and sheepish.

My room was next to the doctor's and she had come

in once or twice, once for a box of matches and some other time for a similar reason, and stayed for a word or so about the climate and the work. But she had always been extremely gruff and casual; so that I was surprised, on the evening in question, to find her sitting on the foot of my bed when I retired. For a moment I thought that she might have come to me as a kind of half-way house with a message of apology to the chief. Not really that her speech had been rude enough to warrant that, but her shrug and her stare and her silence had been, I couldn't help feeling, intentionally offensive. But she began almost as soon as I had closed the door on quite another subject.

'Have you got any influence over Mrs. Pether, Miss Argent?'

'I don't know. Why do you ask?'

'I've tried him. He's a poor sap, by the way, don't you think, to bring her here and then let that happen? And I've tried talking to her, but I can't make either of them see that this is no place for a woman of thirty-seven to have her first baby. Do you think that as a woman and a disinterested party you could make her show a little sense?'

'Where would you have her go?' I asked.

'Somewhere within reach of a good hospital. And somewhere where her nerves could get steady beforehand.'

'What's wrong with her nerves?'

'She's lived in constant terror since, oh, possibly a year ago.'

'Terror of what?'

'Tonga, or his like.'

'How on earth can you tell that?' I was unwillingly remembering that it was almost exactly a twelve-month since we had first heard Tonga's name.

'She turns a horrid chalky colour every time he's mentioned. And I've told her this, so it's no secret – unless I'm very much mistaken she's in for a rough passage. And I've nothing here but the very barest necessities.'

'I see. Of course I'm sorry for her, especially if what you fear is true. All the same, she wouldn't leave Arthur; and I do think that a woman's place is with her husband.'

'You don't. I don't suppose you've ever given the matter a moment's thought. After all, you've never had to, have you?'

It was a second or two before I came to a full realization of her meaning, and when I did I was very angry.

'It may only be your awkward manner,' I said, 'but you've certainly managed to say exactly the wrong thing to everyone in this station. You told Miss Clark that her skin trouble only needed a little common sense and a regular laxative; you've suggested that you know more about Florrie than Arthur does; your whole attitude is an insult to the chief; and I suppose the only thing you can throw at me is my celibacy.'

I ended on a very high note and out of breath. I thought that meeting her with a bluntness equal to her own might take her aback a little; but no, she merely shrugged her shoulders again and said scornfully:

'I don't understand you; you're all supposed to be transparent-minded and straightforward Christians; you wince every time I say "bloody", and yet you're consumed with humbug. The Clark girl does eat too much farinaceous food and neglect her inside, Pether's unworldliness is bordering on the insane, and you can't possibly know anything about obligations of husbands and wives. Why mind admitting any of these things? And for God's sake disabuse yourselves of the idea that I'm trying to insult you. I wouldn't be bothered.'

She flung open my door and strode through it without looking at me again.

Next day, apparently, she approached Miss Andrews upon the question of getting Mrs. Pether sent away, and the argument ended in a really open row. They were alone at the time, so it was only by things said later that we learned that the doctor had accused the chief of being unwilling to lose Florrie's services in the school until the last possible moment; and that Miss Andrews had retorted by accusing her of masquerading as a doctor and then funking her first confinement case. The chief wrote that evening to the secretary-in-charge, begging her to send another doctor if one could be had anywhere. She went so far as to suggest that she was willing to provide another ten per cent on the salary if a suitable Christian person could be found. But before that rash offer could be even commented upon a great many things had happened in Pi Lung.

First of all there was an epidemic in the town. It may have had a special name, but I never heard it; I only remember Dr. Cartwright saying that it was akin to the bad influenza epidemic that went through Europe in 1918. That didn't, I am sorry to say, impress me as being very serious. But it was, they died and died; for three weeks Miss Clark, Arthur Pether, the chief, and the doctor and I went to bed in turns and got up in obedience to the alarm clock after about three hours' sleep. Poor Florrie fretted at not being able to do much, for she had got beyond being able to walk into the town proper, and the school just closed itself because of the sickness. All she could do was to have ready some hot food and a change of clothing for us when we came home.

By the end of the three weeks there were two days without any fresh cases; in another three days the worst sufferers had either died or rounded the corner, and we were beginning to promise ourselves a few lazy days, full of protracted sleeps. There came the day when we all, as usual, met at supper, and I was able to observe the way in which my colleagues had worn. I gave the prize to Miss Andrews. There were tired lines around her eyes and she had lost a little of her naturally high colour, but she looked like a woman who had had a tiring day and would be put right by a good night's rest; but Arthur, Miss Clark, and the doctor looked half dead. We were all beyond talking, sentences begun trailed off half-finished and one by one the dishes of the celebration supper were picked over and sent away. Suddenly the doctor lifted her head from her hands and said with an effort:

'What we want is a good stiff drink all round.'

She got up from the table as if she had been disjointed, stretched, and walked to the door. Miss Andrews's voice, ominously quiet, said: 'What do you mean by a stiff drink, Dr. Cartwright?'

'Generally I mean whisky and soda in more or less equal proportions, but tonight I mean in very unequal proportions.' It was the most weary voice I have ever heard, not much above a whisper and very hoarse. I found time to wish that the chief would at least refrain from baiting her now.

'Kindly don't bring it to this table, if that was your intention. I resent the suggestion being made to my staff in any case.'

I have heard that working together through difficulty and danger engenders friendship between people even of opposite natures; but these two who had been worried and overworked in the same cause were now glaring at each other with nothing less than hatred.

'As you will,' muttered the doctor; 'anybody who thinks it a good suggestion is welcome in my room for five minutes.' Nobody went, which may be a pity – for we could at least have poured the stuff into the plant pots on the window-seat and so diminished the supply that Dr. Cartwright would not have had sufficient to keep her drunk for two whole days. For drunk she was, even at supper on the second day; and it was then that she and the chief had their final meeting and the doctor went from the dining-room to pack her bag.

That scene is graved upon my mind for ever. I stayed with Miss Andrews, who had broken down in tears as

Dr. Cartwright slammed the door. I said that she was wrong to upset her so. We had all had a trying time, but the doctor's was naturally the heavier task, and I imagined that her nervous system was less reliable than ours. Then I, too, crawled to my room. Her door was half open and through the space I could see her standing, wrapped in a dressing-gown, with her hands in her pockets, staring out of the window. Without turning she called me.

'Come here, Miss Argent, and look at this.'

I looked through the window and saw, going straight up into the evening sky, the smoke as it were of an enormous bonfire, about twenty miles away amongst the hills.

'You know what that means?'

'I'm afraid not.'

'Well, I'm afraid I do. That's Tonga. I heard about him in the town today.'

'Oh, no!'

'I'm sure. The barber told me. Some people, he said, were getting out of the town, but there was a general feeling that he wouldn't get as far as this – Tonga, I mean. He will, though.'

'What makes you say that?'

'Several things. There's nothing to stop him. He knows from the Komcha affair that as long as he confines his activities to these towns at the foot of the hills and doesn't cross the river, the Government won't give a damn what he does. Also, and this counts more with me, I've got a sneaky feeling round my heart, as the songs say. And oh, my Lord, what will the silly little Pether do now, poor thing?'

Desperately scared as I was myself I could not help noticing the change in her manner. Ten minutes before, if not actually drunk, she had been quarrelsomely tipsy. Possibly the chief was still weeping in the dining-room over the things that had been said to her. Now she was calm and sensible, and indescribably lightened in manner. Her voice that had been like the dying croak of a run-down gramophone was strong and even less gruff than usual.

'What are we going to do?' I asked, and strangely enough I expected a helpful answer.

'Tell the others, I suppose; and then try to get all the people whose houses face the other way to let us have any horse or donkey they happen to possess, and "silently steal away". You'd better tell the old woman.'

I seemed to have been out of the dining-room for a lifetime, but Miss Andrews was sitting where I had left her and the clock had measured nine minutes exactly. I noticed that particularly, without wishing to. And from the moment I had told her all that Dr. Cartwright said, my mind began, as if in defence, to register only the trivial. I noticed how the chief's hands went helplessly up to her throat, and her lips began to quiver again. I saw the doctor run across the courtyard to the room where the Pethers slept.

'We must do something at once,' the chief gasped at last and her hands dropped, her lip steadied, and she became her usual competent self, as if that moment of weakness had never been. I said nothing, but through the window I saw that Arthur had come down in answer to the doctor's call, and that they stood talking outside while Florrie asked from the window what was the matter. I could see but not hear Dr. Cartwright say: 'Nothing much.' Arthur went off through the gate. The two women exchanged a few words and then the doctor followed him.

'Arthur knows,' I said; 'he's gone into the town, he'll find out whether there's really any danger and whether we can do anything.'

We sat together and waited. There was nothing to do. We did not replenish the fire, and the room turned deadly cold. After a long time a hurried step came past the window and for a second the dark room grew darker still with the passing of a shadow. The next moment the door flew open and Dr. Cartwright stood there, breathless, with her hair tumbling about her face. She held her right hand on her left arm above the elbow and never moved it during the whole of the time we were talking.

'Try to be steady both of you, I've bad news. They've shot Arthur Pether.'

'Who? Why? And Florrie – oh, my God!'

'Tonga's men. They're in the town already, some of them. They'd raided a house and had got the girls. They were screaming. I told him not to interfere, he couldn't do anything. But he went sort of mad. They shot him, just casually. He was quite dead, I made sure of that, and then I ran like hell. I don't want her to know.'

'Poor Arthur! To die like that. How can she help but know? Oh dear, how terrible! How terrible!'

We had all been fond of Arthur; he was a likeable man. For a few moments we forgot that we too were in danger, and felt only sorrow. We were brought back by the doctor's voice saying harshly:

'We shall have to keep it from her until after Sunday; the baby is due then. If only we could keep the whole thing from her – but they're fairly certain to come here. Which reminds me, if you have anything you want to preserve, Miss Andrews, you'd better let me dig it in for you. Records or anything, I mean,' she said impatiently, for the chief was looking at her stupidly. 'I don't suppose that we are in any danger ourselves, but papers and things might easily get lost.'

'What are you going to tell Mrs. Pether?' I asked.

'That Arthur has gone south for help. That'll satisfy her until the baby's born, and after that she won't take it so hard. I judge that she is a rather primitive little woman to whom a baby will mean a great deal. Anyhow, that's the tale until I tell her otherwise. I'm going to her now. Miss Clark has been with her and she knows nothing, which will make it easier. And now, if I were you, I should go to bed. I'll give you both a sleeping-draught if you like.'

'Thank you, I never touch them,' said Miss Andrews. I said nothing, but long after, when I heard Dr Cartwright come to her room, I went and asked her for the tablet she had promised.

'You're not worried, are you?' she asked me. 'There's nothing more than a temporary inconvenience involved.'

'Arthur's was more than that, wasn't it?'

'Well, yes. But he did interfere, and that all happened in the heat of the moment. Tomorrow Tonga himself will most likely be here and there'll be some order again. You see, eventually there'll be England to answer to for anything that happens to us, especially as we have had no part in their politics, and so on. I shouldn't worry if I were you.'

I noticed as she opened her case for the tablets that she was not using her left hand at all. An idea struck me.

'Did you get hurt yourself?' I asked.

'The slightest bit possible; I've done it up and it's quite all right, honestly. Good night, sleep well.'

I did sleep, too well; I was awakened by a soldier who shook me roughly and informed me that Tonga had come and that we were all under arrest. I dressed with great haste and was hurried into the courtyard, where I found the others, their faces pale in the grey light.

Dr. Cartwright had her bag in one hand, a folded blanket over her shoulder and her right arm through Mrs. Pether's. Later on, when I saw her 'slightest possible' wound, I realized what holding the bag must have cost her and how far it accounted for the sickly pallor of her face. The pallor contrasted oddily with her manner; she greeted me cheerily:

'Morning, Miss Argent. We're being carted off for ransom. How much do you think you're worth to the

Daily Postbag?' Never in my life have I felt less cheerful, but I replied, more for Mrs. Pether's sake than for anything else:

'Far less than my cab fare from here to Komcha or wherever we're going. Somebody ought to warn him that he's wasting his time.'

'There's himself,' said the doctor, 'you can tell him.'

I looked at the man who had entered the yard as I was speaking and the strongest shudder of repulsion that I have ever known ran through me, leaving me with a numbness of the hands and feet. As a child I had been haunted by an idea of what Satan would look like, but that imaginary visage was lovely compared with that on which my actual eye now rested in fascinated horror. Half of it had been cut or shot away; there was no cheek on that side, but the mouth was drawn up and the eye down as if to fill the space. His eyelids were red, swollen, and without lashes; beneath them glittered eyes for all the world like specks of coal. The men standing around the courtyard seemed to stiffen as he came in, and I guessed then, what I became certain of later, that they were all terrified of their leader. As well they might be. He had on a sheepskin coat, very roughly made with the fleece inside. It added to his bulk so that he looked like a rolled-up carpet moving towards us on its end. I had a horrible notion that he would touch us, perhaps search for valuables, and I knew that if that fat dirty hand was laid on me I should scream. But he stopped within a yard or two of us and said: 'English?' We nodded vigorously. 'Mission?' We nodded again. My tongue, I know, was paralysed and I thought that those of the others were in a like state. When the doctor said to me: 'Hold Mrs. Pether a moment,' it was as much as I could do to walk across the three feet or so between us. Dr. Cartwright freed her arm and stepped towards Tonga; she had evidently found her tongue.

'You can't do this, Tonga; it won't be the Chinese

Government you'll have to answer to, you know. It'll be England. You'll find that it'll pay you to keep out of the Mission grounds and leave us alone.'

Obviously he did not undertand any of this, though he recognized isolated words.

'Tonga,' he said, pointing to his chest and then at us. 'English Mission. Much money.'

The doctor shook her head and said in the halting faulty patois that had served her at the clinic:

'No money. Not a cash. Only trouble, great trouble.'

'Money first,' said Tonga. 'Trouble can wait.'

'Isn't it a comfort to think that Arthur has gone for help?' Mrs. Peter gasped. 'I don't think I could have borne it.'

'The day of tribulation,' said Miss Andrews, 'When ye shall say to the hills "cover me". That great and terrible day.'

For the first time I became aware of her, and of something strange in her face. It was a vagueness, a placidity, as if the shock had stunned her beyond the realization of what had shocked her. While I looked at her and at Miss Clark, sobbing beside her, Tonga had turned on his heel and was speaking to the men at the gate. They threw it open and called. In response to the call a wagon drew up outside and the men who had been standing like statues on the steps of the house ran forward and began to hustle us towards the gate. We did not wait for any urging, but scrambled into the wagon as quickly as we could, pulling Florrie with us. Half the contents of old Ah Set's silk store was already tumbled upon the floor of the wagon, and Dr. Cartwright said: 'Bless the old brigand, here's a lovely bed for you, Mrs. Pether.'

But a spring mattress could have done little to mitigate the discomfort of that journey. The road between Pi Lung and Komcha was not used for wheeled traffic more than about twelve times in a year and it ran uphill all the way, so that the wagon moved very slowly and often tilted backward. We had difficulty in keeping from falling on top of one another in the lower end of the wagon. Two of Tonga's men sat at the back, dangling their legs over the end and smoking expensive cigarettes that had evidently been part of the loot.

We talked very little. Miss Clark cried herself into a state of exhaustion despite Mrs. Pether's assurances that Arthur would be coming back in two days at most. It was pathetic to hear the faith in the poor little woman's voice and all the time to know. . . . Once the doctor said, thoughtfully:

'It wouldn't be hard to muffle those two fellows in some of that silk and hop down before the ones in front knew anything about it. Only we don't know our way, and it might mean several days' wandering about the hills. And that is not to be thought of.'

The back of the wagon was the only open space, and I don't think any of us was very much interested in looking out under the flapping canvas; but soon after noonday Dr. Cartwright said 'Hullo, we're not going to Komcha. We're turning west.' After that the road rapidly became worse and Mrs. Pether began to lose her spurious courage and to whimper when a more than usually severe jolt shook us. Then Miss Andrews lost patience and said sharply:

'Try to exercise a little control, Florrie. Things like this are sent to try us. It may be for our sins, or for our tolerance of others' sins, that we are made as grain upon the threshing floor.' She looked at the doctor as she spoke of tolerance towards sin, and I knew then that she regarded her as the Jonah in our boat. Dr. Cartwright said nothing, but tried to ease Mrs. Pether as well as she could by rearranging the bales of silk.

Before nightfall the wagon stopped at a lonely house. In obedience to our guards' grunts and signs we got down stiffly and were shepherded into an outbuilding, which had housed poultry not long before, smelt evilly, and, we soon discovered, was full of fleas; but for a moment it seemed a haven of rest after the wagon. Two soldiers stood at the door while the woman of the house brought us a little bean meal, moistened with water, and some greyish-looking goat's milk. Our request for at least a little straw for bedding was either not understood or ignored. The door was shut; we heard various heavy objects rolled against it, and the men went away, leaving us in darkness.

'This is the end,' wailed Miss Clark. 'No bed, no food – not what you could call food – no water to wash in; and Heaven knows what will happen in the morning.' At this Florrie began to cry too and Dr. Cartwright said fiercely:

'I know what will happen to you right away if you don't shut up. It's no worse for you than for anyone else, and there are five of us all together – not like being alone. And people have lain out in shell-holes full of water for days, wounded. Think of that for a bit.'

I could hear her fumbling round the place. 'We'd better lie down, though the floor is damned dirty. We can keep our heads out of it, if I put my head on my bag, and then Miss Argent can put her head on my hips, and Miss Andrews leans on her, and so on. Mrs. Pether can be last.' There was a great deal of scrambling and admonishing before we got ourselves into position, and a great deal of wriggling before we found one unbruised portion on which to lie. Once or twice the doctor laughed outright and even Mrs. Pether giggled feebly. Finally, when we were settled, Miss Andrews remembered that she had not prayed, nor had any of us, so we got up again and repeated the evening prayers as we had each night in the little church. That all seemed very far away; and for perhaps the first time the words 'Deliver us from evil', 'lighten our darkness', and 'bring us to a safe lodging' were real prayers to us.

When I awoke, a faint grey light was streaming in at the top and bottom of the ill-fitting door, and, since our sleeping arrangements had made us form a rough circle, the first thing upon which my eyes lighted was the doctor. She was leaning on her elbow staring at the filthy mud wall in front of her; and there was an expression of such despair upon her face as I had never before seen upon any countenance. Mrs. Pether, with her head on the doctor's stomach, was sleeping soundly. I moved my arm, which was tingling with pins and needles, and she turned her face to me:

'Did you sleep?'

'Splendidly.'

'Miss Andrews isn't leaning on you now, is she? Do you think that, if I wriggled out of this, you could wriggle in without waking her? I want to do my arm up before they're all awake.'

Mrs. Pether stirred and mumbled, but we managed the exchange; I lay and watched the girl take off the bandage and the blood-soaked pad, and I winced long before she said, under her breath, but vehemently:

'Blast the bloody thing.'

One by one they woke and I saw the peaceful look of sleep replaced by one of dismay and anxiety as they realized their position. We heard the men stirring about outside. Another day had begun, and, as Miss Clark had said, only Heaven knew what it had in store for us.

During the afternoon Tonga and some of his men overtook us; he reined up for a moment, exchanged shouts with our driver, and galloped on. That night we did not stop until long after dark; and when we did, it was not at a solitary farmhouse, but in a small town. We could hear people and see lights moving about. Once more we got down and stretched our cramped legs; once more we were herded like cattle through various doorways, and at last through one into a room that had as foul a smell as the one where we had stayed the night before. One of the men carried a lamp, and by its smoky light we could see that the room had nothing in it except some dirty straw. It was lighted and ventilated by some holes in the top of the door. The walls were of plaster and indescribably filthy, the floor of stamped earth. This place had the additional horror of threatening to be more than a temporary stopping-place, and we gazed at one another in disgust, hesitating upon the threshold. The men began to push us.

'I want to see Tonga,' said Dr. Cartwright to the man with the lamp.

'That is impossible until the morning. He is in bed and busy,' said the man.

'It doesn't matter where he is, I must see him. It is very important to him.'

'Only one thing is important to him now,' he said, and walked to the door.

A second later another man arrived with some chunks of rye bread and some water. This he set on the floor, our guide put down his lantern beside the food, and the door bolts shot home. Then for a few minutes there was a moment of pure panic. Miss Andrews threw herself upon her knees and began to pray audibly, while the rest of us, except the doctor, were weeping and wiping our red eyes on our dirty hands. Fortunately perhaps, we were so exhausted by our anxiety and the journey that even the exertion of crying was too great and we fell silent quite suddenly. And in the little lull Dr. Cartwright said:

'Let's make haste over this grub, I want to put out the lantern.'

'Why?'

'I may want it in the night,' she said softly, with a glance at Mrs. Pether.

'Have you a match?' I asked.

'About ten in a box. Lousy supply, I grant you, but it'll do.'

We ate our supper quickly, lay down as before, but with little bundles of straw under our hips and shoulders, and slept. I was awakened by cries and startled voices and a sudden flare of light.

'It's all right, my dear,' Dr. Cartwright's voice said quite calmly, 'it's a couple of days too soon – that's the wagon, I should say. And I'm here. You'll be all right.' We were all awake and, except Mrs. Pether, on our feet by this, and the lantern had begun to shed a clearer light.

That scene was like a nightmare. I had seen one or two babies born, but there had always been a bed of some sort and a supply of hot water; and I think that poor Florrie's would have been a difficult case even under ideal conditions. Indian women, I have been told, have their babies on mud floors and heaps of filthy rags, but outside of India I should think the scene is without fellow. The hours of the night passed slowly, the holes in the door became visible, then the lantern paled and it was morning – and still the baby was not born. Florrie lay and writhed and cried out upon a bed made of our coats. I had seen the bulge of the bandage under the sleeve of the doctor's sweater as she had added her coat to the heap.

A man came with our breakfast at last. Like the supper of the night before it consisted of bread and water.

'I must have hot water,' said the doctor to the man who brought it.

'You have what you have,' he said.

'I want to see Tonga,' she went on.

'He is not yet awake.'

'Then wake him.' At this the man lifted up his hands, shook his head, expressed the uttermost horror.

'Show me the way, I'll wake him. I must see him,' she persisted. The man again shook his head, and suddenly she lost patience and made a dart into the passage outside the door. The man caught her, they swayed for an instant, and then she was thrown heavily upon the floor and the door thrust to behind her.

She picked herself up, looking ruefully at her dirty hands.

'They were filthy enough before,' she said. 'Will you

drink what you want and leave me the rest to wash in.' She washed her hands, when we had all sipped a drop or two of the water, and dried them on her skirt.

At about ten o'clock Miss Andrews put her hands to her ears and gasped:

'Stop it for pity's sake! Haven't you any chloroform in that bag?'

'Yes, I have, and I know when to use it.'

That was the only time she snapped during the whole business. Half an hour later she did use the chloroform, and in the following calm the baby was born. We cleansed it as well as we could and wrapped it in bits of underclothing that we could spare. It was a boy, rather a fine baby; we took turns, Miss Andrews, Miss Clark, and I, in sitting on the floor and holding him. Until you have tried it you have no idea how difficult it is for a person accustomed to chairs to sit on the bare floor for any length of time.

Midday passed and no one came near us. Some time in the afternoon the baby began to wail feebly and the doctor came from Florrie's corner and said fiercely:

'Unless something is done the poor brat will die; she has no milk, and even if we get our supper it'll be no good to him.'

She eyed the door for a second and then took a running leap at it, caught two fingers of each hand through the holes at the sides, and put her mouth to the one in the middle. Through the hole she began to shout 'Oy's' and 'Hi's' and the name Tonga, mingled with the foulest abuse in both English and Chinese that she could lay her tongue to. Presently someone came running and she had only time to let go her hold and drop to her feet before the door was thrown open. Two men stood in the opening.

'I must see Tonga,' she said, in a voice that contrasted strangely with her frantic yelling.

'Very well,' said one of the men, and then one seized

her by one arm, one by the other, and slamming the door, they hustled her off.

Even deeper gloom settled down on our dungeon. The baby went on wailing and Florrie began to moan too.

'She'll never come back, you'll see. They'll tell him what she called him and he'll have her killed or shut up underground or something. Then the baby will die and so shall I – and Arthur will never see either of us.'

She went on and on in this strain. We tried to calm her, to hush the baby, and to hold our cold arms with our hands. We were now no more than half-clad, what with giving our coats to Florrie and our petticoats to the baby; and the clay walls and mud floor seemed to send out waves of dampness as well as evil odours.

After about two hours that seemed as long as two years, we heard steps in the passage, and the doctor came in unhustled. One of the men following her was carrying a rolled-up mattress and a rug, and the other was holding a pan of warm milk with both hands. They set down these things, took away the exhausted lantern, brought in another, and shut the door. The doctor was already dipping a fragment of Miss Clark's petticoat into the milk and holding it to the baby's mouth. The wailing changed to little sucking noises, and after the rag had been redipped several times, the doctor put the baby into my arms and, taking up the pan, went to Florrie.

'Here you are, Mrs. Pether – some milk heated for you over Tonga's own fire; there's an honour!'

We burst out into a storm of questions. We gathered from her answers that Tonga expected to get five hundred pounds for each of us; that he was entirely impervious to threats, and that the milk and the mattress were only gained by cajolery of the most abject nature. 'Still,' she said, 'I would have licked his boots at that moment for a little milk; fortunately he didn't happen to think of it.'

Presently our supper arrived; and, though by this time the sight and smell of our room would have been calculated to turn the stoutest stomach, we found ourselves devouring our beans with gusto. Florrie having been moved on to the mattress and covered by the two rugs that we now had and the baby laid beside her, we were at liberty to put on our coats again. I can hardly remember any experience that has given me such piercing pleasure as the feel of my coat, warm from Florrie's body, sliding over my frozen arms.

Next morning early with our breakfast, came a message that Tonga wished to see the doctor. She got up from the side of Mrs. Pether's bed, put her left hand into her pocket with a gesture of pain, and brushed down her skirt with the right.

'Command performance,' she muttered. 'I'll be odd if I can't get some hot water and at least a blanket apiece out of this.'

The men did not seize her arms this time, but stood in the doorway as she went through.

Early in the afternoon the steps were heard again and the door opened. The same two men entered, but they were alone and carried a rough stretcher. They proceeded to lift Mrs. Pether on to this and signed to Miss Clark, who stood nearest, to pick up the baby.

'Follow,' they said, and we did so – along the passage, up some steps, and into an archway. Here the one who was walking first set down his end and unlocked a door. We followed the stretcher in and found two little rooms, clean compared with the one we had left, each lighted by a small window. One of the rooms contained a mattress, and when the men had put down the stretcher, one of them went out and returned with the bedding and rugs which had been left behind. They then locked the door and went away.

'Well, this is better,' I said, 'but where is Dr. Cartwright?'

'If I could only manage a wash,' sighed Miss

Andrews. But apparently, if Tonga had listened to and understood a request for a bed and rather more space, he was not in sympathy with any extravagant ideas of cleanliness. Our supper came and we had laid down, for want of something better to do, on the unwontedly comfortable resting-place of half a straw paillasse each. We had fed the baby on the milk that came with our food and he had been quiet for a time, so that we were dropping asleep when the door opened and the doctor came in.

'Where have you been all day? How did you manage this?' we asked. But she began to fuss over Florrie, and not until she had finished with her and examined the baby did she say, casually:

'Oh, I've been riding with Tonga.'

'With Tonga?'

'Ummmm. We've spent the day exchanging compliments. I am as beautiful, according to him, as Ting-a-ling-ling or somebody like that, and I called him a Chinese Paul Jones. We both understand about one word in ten, but that serves.'

'I can't think how you can bear to look at him,' I said with feeling.

'I don't look at him. I've been looking at Florrie all day,' she said queerly. And just then the baby began to cry. The doctor picked him up, and he was sick all over her coat.

'Hell,' she said, not referring to the mishap, I felt. 'It's their lousy dirty milk; and I've nothing at all for a sick baby, all that stuff was in the clinic. Poor little devil, what a beginning!' She squeezed a few drops of water into the tiny mouth, then laid the wailing gulping baby beside his mother and wiped her sleeve on her filthy handkerchief.

'What does it say about never seeing the righteous forsaken or his seed begging bread? I suppose the milk is another matter.'

She went to the door and tapped on it. It opened immediately; obviously someone had been awaiting the signal.

'Where are you going?'

'Command performance, ten-thirty precisely,' she said grimly and the door shut.

For a long while I could not sleep. The baby kept crying and Florrie cried and endeavoured to hush it. Miss Andrews voiced her disapproval of this new move; Miss Clark said that no doubt she knew what was best for her – the doctor, I mean – and I found myself losing my temper in her defence.

Confinement, anxiety, and discomfort had frayed all our tempers, and perhaps we were even glad of a quarrel to relieve the monotony.

'I dare say,' Miss Andrews said to me, 'she enjoys posing as a martyr and considers that she has gained us this slight relief by behaving like a scarlet woman; but I think it would better have become us to have remained together and suffered until it pleased God to let this cup pass from us. Nothing soiled can be His instrument.'

Finally the baby cried itself to sleep and one by one the others fell silent, but still I lay awake wondering. I thought of Miss Andrew's bitter words and was, secretly, shaken. Perhaps the doctor had found herself a way out of this misery, perhaps she did not find Tonga repulsive; but from that my mind turned away. Impossible to imagine a woman depraved enough to go to him of her own free will.

For three days longer we waited. The baby was very ill. Florrie gained no strength; how could she on a little milk twice a day? Sometimes the baby kept down his share of the milk; more often he was sick, and almost all his waking hours he was crying. Florrie and Miss Clark were almost as bad and Miss Andrews seemed to be going crazy. Nearly the whole of her conversation was quotations from the Bible or long, involved prayers. There are some prayers that I have never been able to listen to with equanimity since. Twice a day the doctor came in, each day more ill and distracted looking. On the third evening she picked up the baby in one hand and the lantern in the other and looked hard at him.

'Isn't there anything you can do?' sobbed Florrie. 'I feel I would carry him to a hospital or something if I could only get out.'

'You won't have to do that,' said the doctor, giving her back the baby.

'Why, have you heard from Arthur? Is help coming?' Even Miss Andrews and Miss Clark, who had ostentatiously turned their faces to the wall as the 'scarlet woman' entered, pricked their ears for the answer.

'You'll see.'

She went away thoughtfully, nursing her arm.

About four hours later I awoke to find a light shining in my face and the doctor shaking me by the shoulder. Even at that moment I noticed the long green earrings glittering under her red hair and the smear of red on her lips. She left me and I opened my eyes, and went to the bed where Miss Clark and the chief were sleeping. I saw her look at them for a moment with an impish expression on her face; then she reached down and shook them, one after the other. Florrie was already wrapping the baby in a rug.

'Take the baby, Miss Argent; and all of you come after me, as quick as you can and as quietly.'

She thrust her arm through Florrie's, then withdrew it as Florrie reeled and put her arm completely round her waist, keeping the lantern in her left hand. We went down the stairs, along the passage where our first room was, and then on, turning about a way I did not remember. Finally we came to a gate which opened at a touch. Outside stood a cart, much smaller and lighter than the one in which we had come. A man who stood beside it looked at us without interest until the doctor spoke, but then came forward and helped to lift Florrie into the vehicle. 'There are several cushions, and it won't be such a bad road this way. You can trust the man; Tonga was going to have his head off tomorrow morning.'

'Aren't you coming?' I asked, astounded.

'Can't. He's dead drunk, asleep, but he'll wake before morning. I shall go to your room as usual tomorrow with the men and take in the breakfast. At night he can do what he likes; you'll all be safe by then.'

'But you?' I said.

By way of answer she lifted her left hand. It was extremely swollen and discoloured. I looked at her neck and saw the enormously enlarged glands throbbing.

'I shall last long enough to take the breakfast, I trust, and not much more. Don't let that worry you. Break it gently about Arthur, won't you?'

She nodded to the driver, who picked up his whip. I saw through the tears that were pouring down my face the lonely figure at the gate, the Chinese coat – evidently Tonga's present – gleaming in the lanternlight. I thought of the poison being carried with every beat of her pulses. . . . I knew that I should never speak to Miss Andrews again.